Bottom Line Publications

Presents

Marry

Me

Or

Live

In

Misery

<u>A NOVEL BY</u>

Eric Lamont Williams

ISBN: 9798601802147

Edited By: Eric Lamont Williams

Cover By: Iesha Bree "coversmyway.com"

Facebook: Bottom Line Publications LLC (PLEASE FOLLOW)

Email: ericw8403@gmail.com

ACKNOWLEDGMENTS

First, I would like to thank God for giving me the knowledge, encouragement, wisdom and dedication to write this book. I still remember starting my first book and now I'm starting my fourth one, that just shows you with determination you can accomplish whatever you want. I want to thank everyone who has supported me in my journey of writing. With a special shout out to my mother and my sister Tajuanda.

I would like to also give shout outs to everyone pursuing their dreams, which is not an easy thing to do with all the negativity and haters out here. None of you should let nothing stop your journey because you are the only one who can achieve your dreams so go for it no matter what. To everyone who has purchased my previous books and are reading the words of this book right now I want to say thanks to all of you, without you there would be no me. All the rest of my family and friends I would like to thank all of you as well.

Rest in peace to all my deceased family and friends. I would also like to say rest in peace to all of yours as well because death is a sad thing when it's someone you love. Like they say though "God made His hardest battles for his strongest soldiers." Get ready to read this book as it will take your mind to a level it has never been. Thanks!!!

INTRODUCTION

"Check mate my nigga," said Dizzy as he closed in on Dunkin's king with his rook for the check mate on the Chess board.

"Man, nigga you got me fucked up I was just seeing how far you was going to go. You cheated because when I came back from serving Draco that nine piece you had moved my pieces," said Dunkin.

Everybody knew that Dunkin hated losing with a passion and would never take his defeat like a man, so everyone got used to him complaining like a little woman. Most people wouldn't even play against him in anything because all he did was make excuses when he lost. Dizzy had been Dunkin's best friend since grammar school, so he knew of his ways very well. Though Dunkin had grew up getting beat up and chased off the bus everyday he turned into a hell of a guy. He took no time climbing to the top and had no hesitation when it came time to killing a nigga who stepped on his toes in the drug game. Dizzy had been there with him through it all and had never turned his back on him. That's why they were sitting on Dunkin's mother's screened in porch and his mother had no problem with it. Dizzy could even be there alone because he grew up like her second son. None of Dunkin's other friends knew where she lived.

Though Dunkin was getting beat up and chased off the bus in his school years his mother nor his father missed a beat in his life. He grew up spoiled and that was part of the reason he thought he was always supposed to have his way as an adult. His mother was still a thick and beautiful white woman even at the age of fifty-two. Dunkin's father was black and though a player in the past he was still with Dunkin's mother and had no plans of leaving her ever. Dunkin's mother Chelly still turned heads every time she left the house and his father still got jealous every time. Dunkin's father couldn't see no one else being with Chelly so he stayed put. Dunkin's father had retired from Pepsi and now had his own independent routes for Pepsi on the side while still collecting his retirement money. Chelly was a retired RN and she also invested into many other business ventures on the side. Overall Chelly probably doubled her husband's worth, but she still treated him like a king. That was another reason he would never leave her side. Dunkin's father's name was Deacon. He was raised in church and that's where his name originated from because his father was a deacon.

Deacon was the only man Dunkin would listen to in the world other than his personal fitness trainer Eric, though he only halfway listened to either of them. Dunkin's father used to always tell him the enjoyment of having one woman in his life, but Dunkin wasn't hearing none of that. Dunkin waited to turn eighteen years old so he could take his money from a trust fund his parents started for him. His parents started his trust fund the day they found out his mother was pregnant. With all the interest and money his parents put in Dunkin collected over a million dollars from his trust fund. When he cashed in his trust fund, he turned into something no one ever knew he would. He turned into a money getting womanizing savage.

Dunkin bought a brick of heroin and five bricks of cocaine when he first entered the game and at the age of thirty-seven, he still had never fell off. He went to the top and made it hard for anyone to get on his level. He invested into some other business ventures, but drugs was his main source of income and his plot was so solid that the police had never had him under their radar. His parents hated he turned into a drug dealer, but they just lived with it because they knew there was nothing, they could do to stop him anyway. Dunkin's only sibling was a girl and she hated Dunkin with a passion because their parents always gave him what he wanted and had his back on whatever. Though Dunkin had a baby mansion with his fiancée he was always at his mother and fathers house. Since his sister Tyrea lived there, she always had to see his face and she hated it. She didn't see that she was spoiled just like he was, at thirty years old she still had never moved out of their parent's house and never paid a bill. All Tyrea did was sit on her money and still had never dated a man. Whenever Tyrea and Dunkin got into an argument, he would always mention that she was still a virgin and needed to go get some dick.

Tyrea was a bad little thick mixed piece. Hands down the coldest chick from their whole neighborhood. Many men were scared to say anything to her because of Dunkin, but when she went to work it was a different story. She had men coming at her from all angles at work. She was an RN just like her mother was and she loved what she did. Tyrea was a lover not a fighter and she made her parents proud to be her parents. Her scrubs did her no justice at all you could still see every curve she had in her body because they were too hard to hide. She stood five foot five and her measurements were a thirty-four, twenty-four, forty. She stayed in LA fitness and eating healthy foods to keep up with her shape. Many women hated on her because she was half white, but she didn't care because she stayed in her own lane. She had been in one fight in her life and she beat the woman so bad that it was still talked about in the hood thirteen years later. Tyrea only fought that time because she had no other choice.

"Nigga you know I didn't cheat you just can't take your loss," said Dizzy as he laughed and started popping his collar in his all red and gold Balmain shirt.

Next thing you knew Dizzy hit the ground and laid their lifeless in a pool of blood.

"I told yo bitch ass you cheated nigga, yo bitch ass got me fucked up," said Dunkin as he held his Glock seventeen on his side.

Dunkin had just murdered his best friend of practically his whole life over a chess game and it didn't seem like he had any remorse about it at the time. He didn't try to go revive his best friend or nothing. Instead he stood there still insulting him and cussing him out as if he was still living. After that his mother and sister came rushing outside not knowing what had just went down on their porch. As soon as they both locked eyes on Dunkin they knew what had happened.

“Dunkin what the hell have you done to your best friend,” asked Chelly as tears started to roll down her face?

Chelly had always been there for Dizzy because both his parents were killed in a car accident when he was still very young. She really felt like Dizzy was a son to her and didn’t like what she had just witnessed. Dunkin was her son but at times she felt like Dizzy had a bigger heart for her than Dunkin. It didn’t matter what time it was Dizzy never refused whatever it was she wanted. He spent every holiday with them and bought nice gifts for everyone.

“Momma this nigga cheated me in Chess and then laughed in my face,” said Dunkin as he paced back and forth like he was still angry even after he had just taken his best friends’ life. His two long braids on his six-foot five-inch body just swung from side to side as he paced the porch in anger.

"I fucking hate you Dunkin. I guess you will end up killing one of us next, I wish I could kick your ass you punk bitch," said Tyrea as she turned around and walked back into the house with a face full of tears and feeling like she was about to vomit.

Tyrea knew in her mind that she would pay Dunkin back for everything he did to everyone else, she didn't care if he was her brother or not. This wasn't the first time Dunkin had killed someone in her presence and she was tired of it. She didn't know why her parents would keep letting him come over knowing what could possibly happen because of his temper and spoiled childish acts of violence.

"Right now, is not the time little bitch you act like you want me to put some dick in you while you always got an attitude with me," said Dunkin talking to his little sister giving her a mug that would make a bitch nigga scared.

"Don't you dare talk to your sister like that Dunkin," said Chelly.

"I hate all you motherfuckers I'm out of here," Dunkin said as he attempted to walk out the porch door.

"No, you're about to sit your ass here and clean up this heartbreaking problem you just created," Chelly said as she took Dunkin's gun out of his hand.

"And how the hell am I going to do that, the police will be pulling up any minute I have to go. Just tell them he pulled up over here shot," said Dunkin as he turned to tried to leave out again.

Before any more words were said, his mother shot him in the shoulder.

"What the fuck did you just do Momma," asked Dunkin as he hollered in pain while dropping to the ground?

"No someone came on this porch trying to rob you both, now lay down before the police come. These police ass neighbors are already lining up in front of the house," said Chelly as she let Dunkin know what to say when the police were to get on the scene.

Chelly then ran in the house and told her Butler to put on all black then run from the front of the house and to not stop running. She told him someone would be calling him in a few minutes to pick him up. Without hesitation he went to his room, threw on all black, and started running. Their Butler would never go against them because they were there for him when no one else would be there for him. They paid him good to keep their house together and run their errands for them. He had a nice bank account and could have his grand children spend the night whenever he wanted. He had not one complaint about anything when it came to his job, so he did whatever was asked of him and more.

Chelly then ran outside crying and cussing at her Butler as he ran off in an act of persuading her neighbors to think it was the shooter running off. Her neighbors rushed to her side to comfort her and she told them that her two sons were shot by whoever the man was that ran off. Next thing you knew the police had the whole street blocked off. The medics checked Dizzy's pulse and marked him dead on the scene then put Dunkin in an ambulance to go to the hospital. The police questioned Chelly and Tyrea first before questioning the neighbors. The police summed up that it was a robbery gone bad after they talked to everyone including Dunkin.

Dunkin was released from Methodist Memorial Hospital the next day. When his mother pulled up to get him, he told her to keep going because he had nothing to say to her ever again. Dunkin felt his mother should have never shot him and to keep from killing her he didn't want her around him. Dunkin called his fiancée Milly to pick him up and waited until she got there. Milly was a cold Mexican piece that Dunkin left his ex-fiancée Candice for, who was a cold ass black chick.

While Dunkin was in the hospital bed his only baby mama NuNu stayed by his side. After all she was the woman, he was with practically all his life and he could do no wrong in her eyes. While lying in the hospital bed Dunkin didn't even think about his best friend who he had just murdered for nothing. After multiple women came to see him, he ended up getting some head from one of the CNA's who was working in the hospital. Dunkin was still his old self like nothing ever happened. Even though he was shitty about his mother shooting him in his shoulder. He kept his fiancée Milly away from the hospital because he knew it would be trouble if she seen all the other women coming to visit him. Milly knew NuNu and knew that she would always be by Dunkin's side, but all the other women were problems. Dunkin didn't even know that the CNA he decided to get head from was a friend of his ex-fiancée Tylia and Tylia was the woman that he left NuNu for, so it was just a weird situation. The CNA knew exactly who Dunkin was and though she was married, she was just like many other women running around Indianapolis with a fantasy of sleeping with Dunkin. Dunkin was the lady's man, and no one could take that from him.

CHAPTER 1

It was just four days after Dizzy's funeral and Dunkin was getting ready for a trip to Jamaica. No one suspected any foul play from Dunkin in the least bit. Dunkin played his part at the funeral and cried in front of a crowd that thought he could never cry. He still wouldn't say a word to his mother. Even after his father told him that his mother did what she had to do to keep him out of jail. Dunkin was too stubborn to get the fact through his head. If it wasn't for his mother's quick thinking there was no way they could have covered up him killing his best friend. Dunkin showed up to the funeral in an all money green three-piece Kiton K-50 suit, with a pair of Salvatore Ferragamo loafers on to match. He even went as far as to have the cast he wore remade in Louis Vuitton by a designer out of California.

Dunkin didn't sit in the front row seats at Dizzy's funeral, instead he sat in the back row with his

Louis Vuitton shades on to hide his tears. No one thought it was out of the ordinary for him to be sitting in the back row because they knew he was going through a lot of emotional pain. Afterall he had just lost his lifetime best friend. Milly sat on his left side while his three children Tamara, Dunkin Jr., and Dexter sat on his right side. His children's mother NuNu sat in the front row with his mother, father, and sister. Most of the time while Dunkin was in the back row, he was playing Spades Plus on his iPhone. From past experiences everyone knew he was weird like that, so it was nothing out of the ordinary. Chelly, Deacon, and Tyrea were the only ones who knew what really went on when Dizzy lost his life. That secret would go with them to their grave, though Tyrea wanted to tell the police on Dunkin.

After Dizzy's burial, NuNu and Milly talked Dunkin into going to the repass with his family. Dunkin still didn't want to go, but after Dizzy's children asked him to go, he felt bad and told them he was going to follow behind them in his own car. Dizzy's children looked at Dunkin like he was their real blood uncle and he looked at them like they were his blood as well. Dunkin had never missed a beat in their lives. He was there for their every accomplishment and their every failure. He was so tight with them that he even went along with Dizzy and their mother to their parent teacher conferences. Just like Dizzy went along with him and NuNu to their parent teacher conferences. Dunkin knew he took the most important person to them away from them and that's what made him feel bad. What no one knew was that Dunkin had taken three hundred thousand dollars from his stash and gave it to Candice. Candice was Dizzy's baby mama and the money was for her to start a trust fund for her and Dizzy's children. Dunkin told her to never mention it to the children until she felt they were old enough to handle the money with care. Dunkin had also been sleeping with Candice for years behind his best friend's back. They both met her together when she stripped at Sunset Strip Club years earlier. Dunkin didn't want her that night, but Dizzy had fell in love with her almost instantly. Dizzy was just a sucker for love like that.

One-night Dunkin was out drunk smashing through the city in his brand-new Camaro and ran into Candice who was accompanied by two of her female friends. Dunkin ended up getting a room that night and slept with all three of them. He ended up getting Candice pregnant that night, but she had an abortion because she knew Dizzy would have known it was Dunkin's baby. The night that Dunkin gave her the money she wanted sex then. Dunkin turned her away because he felt bad about the whole situation, though he did want to dive into her chocolate skin.

Dunkin only had one baby mama, but he did have another child on the way by a Puerto Rican chick named Lisa. No one ever knew how she ended up with a name like Lisa, but they did know that she was one of the coldest women in the city. Lisa hated Dunkin with a passion. Dunkin had played her, and Lisa didn't like that she was played. A few niggas who had played her before had come up missing and with all her heart, she was going to see to it that Dunkin came up missing as well.

Lisa had brothers who were in the game just like Dunkin was who were not afraid of him. They were just smart about the situation because they knew he had money for war, and they didn't have money to spend like that. Lisa on the other hand didn't care about a war and figured she could get Dunkin back in her own way. What made things so much better for her is that she was very good friends with his sister Tyrea. Even though Tyrea never gave her information or even talked about him to Lisa. Lisa was sneaky and able to find out things about him in her own way. Plus, Dunkin's parents would let Lisa come over and walk in their house as if she lived there with them. Milly was jealous of the relationship Lisa and NuNu had with Dunkin's family but knew there was nothing she could do about it.

At the repass Dunkin paid for everything for everyone who came and eventually talked to his mother. Everyone in the house was drinking Remy 1738, D'usse, and Twenty Grand. Along with them smoking some of the best weed in the streets at the time. Dunkin spent a lot of money to be going to a place that he never wanted to go to in the first place. It was starting to set in on him that his best friend was dead, and he was the cause of his death. He knew in his heart that if Dizzy was still alive, they would have been going to Denny's for breakfast that morning as they did every morning. On top of that they would have been clowning on Facetime throughout the day laughing as they always did. Dunkin was finally seeing he did have a heart, after all the murders he had committed he had never felt bad. His feelings was starting to catch up with him though and he felt horrible.

Things did get a little entertaining at the repass when Lisa and her girls shoved their ways into the door and began to attack Milly. That was short lived because Chelly began throwing blows at Lisa and her girls letting them know that they were being some disrespectful hood rats. Though Chelly did have love for Lisa she wasn't going to see anyone get jumped, especially at the repass. She also knew in her heart that her son would have murdered the women right there in front of everyone. Lisa looked at Chelly in disbelief but knew better than to disrespect her.

Dunkin was prepared for his trip to Jamaica. He always liked to travel out of the country alone which made Milly upset, but she let him go in peace knowing he was only going to cheat on her anyway. Over the time of Milly being with Dunkin she had somewhat got used to him cheating. She began to accept his behavior as a behavior she couldn't change and still promised to stay faithful to him. Only thing Milly was waiting on was to be Dunkin's wife thinking marriage would change his behavior. She was upset daily that he cheated on her and got Lisa pregnant though. What Dunkin didn't know is that Milly was pregnant with his baby as well. She knew it would excite him but didn't want to tell him until he came back from Jamaica. She wanted to give him time to get over his best friend dying.

Dunkin was riding with his father headed to Castleton Square Mall to get a few more items for his trip. Deacon was waiting to have another serious conversation with his son. There were some things he wanted to say to Dunkin not caring if Dunkin was to listen or not, he just wanted to tell him. Deacon was a man who loved old school cars. It was no secret that he went all out on his old schools. He was riding in a drop top seventy-two Impala better known as a Donk to car lovers. Deacon drove his drop Impala for a reason that day. He drove it because it always made Dunkin laugh to see his older father driving in a dressed-up car. Deacon had the car for a long time just as an original old school, but Dunkin had taken it from him for a few months and got it totally redone. It went from original white paint to burnt orange paint, from original interior to all Gucci interior, from original rims and tires to thirty-two-inch Forgiato rims, from the original dash to an all-digital dash. To say the least Deacon's Impala was one of the best in the city of Indianapolis. And the 496 chrome Stroker engine made the Impala go from zero to sixty quick.

Deacon always talked to his wife about what he could have done different in Dunkin's life to have made him a better man. She would always tell him that there was nothing he could have done because he had done more than most mothers had even done for their children. She always assured him that he was a great father. She told him to let his daughter be an example that he did raise a successful child. Chelly let him know that Dunkin was a different breed from anyone she had ever seen. She also reminded him that he raised his children to always follow themselves. That was probably the reason why Dunkin didn't listen to no one, but himself. She reminded him that he told his children to stay away from gangs, so he did nothing wrong by raising them to listen to themselves. No matter what Chelly said to Deacon he always beat himself up about his son. He prayed every day and every night that no one would kill his son. In his heart, he knew it would happen soon if Dunkin didn't change his attitude.

Deacon turned down his music and said, "you know your mother and I have tried our best with you, but do you think we have failed you in any way?"

"Old man I've told you repeatedly that both of you have done the best job ever raising me and my sister. Stop beating yourself up about my life pops I love you man," said Dunkin as he looked at his father and started to feel bad. Though Dunkin was a momma's boy he still loved both of his parents just the same and hated to feel like he was the reason for their sadness.

"Son, no matter how old you get you will always be my baby boy. I'm getting old and though my health is good anything can happen to me and I want you to be here with me for the rest of my days," said Deacon.

"I'll be right by your side old man. I just don't know what gets into me sometimes that makes my anger flare up the way it does. I don't know if it's because I always felt like an outsider growing up or what," responded Dunkin.

"I know the feeling son, but you have to find other ways to vent your anger. I almost choked when your mom told me that you had cussed your sister out and called her a bitch. You know we raised you better than that and though you have done things in front of us you have never been the one to really use foul language in front of us," said Deacon.

"It's like nothing really makes me happy anymore old man. Even with all the women I got right now, I still watch Pornhub and jack off about four times a day. And no matter how much money I got I still want more. The clothes I buy don't even make me happy anymore after I buy them. I'm really just lost out here, but I've been doing a lot of thinking," said Dunkin as his eyes drifted into space.

"These things happen in life son. I've been through the same things and still jack off about four times a day myself. Shit I got porn magazines and movies in the trunk right now," said Deacon as they both laughed, and he pushed his son on the shoulder.

After a minute or two of quietness Dunkin said, "you know I'm going to Jamaica now to see if I can find a place so I can move there and leave all this behind. I have a beautiful woman there and everything,

I want to leave everything here behind. Leaving the game, Milly, my kids and all. You, momma, and Tyrea will be the only ones who know my whereabouts if I do move."

"Sounds like a good idea, but you can't just run from your problems Dunkin. If the problem is within you, then you will have the same problems you have here no matter where you go. Can you just take some time while over there on the water to think," asked Deacon?

"It's not just that easy for me pops," replied Dunkin.

"I know, but you're being selfish when you talk about leaving your children behind. Then you probably haven't even told Milly yet. You have to think about other people's feelings too son, you can't just run away only thinking of your own," said Deacon.

"I'll think about it pops. That's why I like talking to you and Eric because both of you give me the real," said Dunkin.

Dunkin had a couple other close friends, but no one was like Dizzy to him. Every time he left the country, he left his friends in charge of everything he had when it came to his street business. Zynika was his female friend and probably one of the only female friends he had that he hadn't slept with. Zynika wasn't for no games in no way. She strutted around Indianapolis like she owned it. She was light skinned, pretty, and had ass for days. She made a lot of money in the streets and was very particular about the men she messed with, just like they were about her. Most men knew Zynika was close to Dunkin and didn't want to mess with her because of him.

On this day Zynika was with the other members of her and Dunkin's crew. What Zynika or none of the rest knew was that Dunkin played them all against each other. He was attempting to make sure no one messed up and make them all watch over each other. Zynika thought she was a secret spy over the other three members. The other three members thought they were spies over the other three members because Dunkin told them all the same story. Dunkin had a way of making no one feel relaxed when it came to business. He would make one person think they had more power than the others, but they were all even when it came to power, he just played with their minds to get what he wanted.

"I hope you two niggas can cover me today because I got some shit to do tonight with my kids," said Zynika talking to Terrance and Draco, though Nicole was there too.

Terrance and Draco would do anything Zynika told them to do because they both wanted to be her man. Zynika turned around in her Adidas yoga pants to let them get a glimpse of her ass. She knew showing her ass would make them fight over who was going to take her shift. Draco and Nicole were siblings while Terrance was just another associate of the crew. They all grew up together at the end of the day and felt they were all blood.

Zynika needed them to cover her because she had to take her children out of town to Ohio to see their father in jail the next day. She knew they wouldn't mind because they all covered for each other when the time was needed. In no way could they let Dunkin know about this though. Dunkin was very strict when it came to them working their shifts. He didn't want none of them covering for each other because that meant the one covering could get tired. Dunkin knew working two shifts could lead to them being sleepy and getting caught slipping on the job. Everyone had their time to be on the clock and there were no sick days in Dunkin's eyes. If they needed time off other than for a family emergency they didn't need to be on his team, that's the way he thought.

"Nik Nik you know I got you," said Draco as he stood there in his all white Polo shorts, white Polo button up, and all white custom-made Jordan's, not to mention his eighty thousand dollar Cuban link necklace flooded in diamonds.

"Naw, I'll do it for her bro, I'm not on shit tonight anyway," Terrance said as he mugged Draco.

"You two bitch ass nigga's better not start arguing about this shit again or I'm a shoot both of you niggas. These niggas be fighting over you every time you say something girl and know good and damn well neither one of them is going to get the pussy," said Nicole as she laughed and gave Zynika a high five.

Over the time they had been in the crew together getting money they all got very close to one another. Zynika would sometimes flirt with Draco and Terrance, but they knew they had no chance of being with her, though it never stopped them from trying. Nicole was cold herself, but she didn't want nothing but another woman. She had a secret no one ever knew about and that was about her and Dizzy sleeping together before he died. They were both drunk and it happened, but both knew it was a mistake and agreed to never tell a soul.

After that Terrance and Draco started slap boxing and wrestling debating about which one of them would be the first to fuck Zynika. They all had separate rooms at the house they were then at for their meeting. It sat in a quiet area on the far east side of Indianapolis. It had five bedrooms, six bathrooms, and a six-car garage. They all put their money into the house, and it was a getaway spot for them all. Only certain people could know about this house and their spouses were not included in those certain people. Their number one rule was that no spouses or close significant others were allowed. They had an indoor swimming pool where they hosted the best parties in the city at, but they only invited people from out of town. It was at one of their pool parties where they all seen Zynika naked when she chose to get drunk, strip down, and jump in the pool. Dunkin didn't want everybody seeing her naked though, so he immediately told her to get back dressed. He was just jealous about it because he always wanted to see her naked alone but could never even get her to unbutton her pants.

CHAPTER 2

Lisa was at her house trying to get a rock-solid plan together to kill Dunkin. She had five niggas with her that was trained to go, she chose them because she felt her brothers feared Dunkin. Though she was pregnant she was still fucking all the niggas as their payment to do what she told them to do. She walked around the house with pink boy shorts and a white tank top on. Her nipples were sticking out from out the sides of the tank top. She had the niggas with her hypnotized like she was their ruler. One thing about Lisa is that she knew the power a woman held when it came to horny niggas and she used it to her ability. Her grandmother was sure to embed the story of Queen Esther in her head and that was where she built her confidence from. Which was another reason why she hated Dunkin so much because she hated the fact that he played her so cold. She thought she had him on lock and then he made her look stupid in front of everybody.

"Nigga you get down and suck my toes, you get over here and lick in this asshole until you taste some shit, and you lick my pussy. You other two goofy motherfuckers get ready for next because I feel freaky," said Lisa as she got up from her chair blowing smoke circles out of her mouth after she hit the blunt.

Just like robots programmed to a certain function they did exactly what Lisa told them to do. Her little feet were so pretty that she could have probably charged a weird nigga money just to lick on them. Lisa stood there looking out her back-patio window smoking her blunt with three men on their knees pleasing her, the only thing on her mind was murder though. Dunkin didn't know what he was in for, but she didn't know what she was in for neither. Lisa had men ready to do anything she told them to do because of her body and looks, but Dunkin's respect came from others fearing him. The upper hand Lisa had was the element of surprise because Dunkin had no idea about her plans.

Some of Lisa's goons were close to Dunkin and many of his associates. She chose people close to Dunkin because she figured that would make it easier for her to have him killed.

Many of Lisa's family members felt she was scorned from what she went through as a child. Though she didn't go through much abuse she seen her mother get abused by her dad daily. Lisa made a promise to herself at a young age to never let a man control her the way her mother was controlled. Her family members knew she was a savage and that she could get anyone killed by just snapping her fingers. She was so beautiful that you would never suspect she was capable of the things she had done in her past or the acts that were soon to come. She had one of her exes beaten to death and beat the case in trial because she had all the witnesses killed right from Marion County Jail. Lisa could rap her ass off and was known for shutting the club down when it came to battle rapping. That's how her and Dunkin really started messing around. Since Dunkin thought he was the coldest rapper and she thought she was too, they would often be at the same places at the same time. After seeing each other so much they started fucking around.

After Lisa was pleased by her goons, she told one of them to go get a bucket and wash her down with soap and water. One thing about Lisa is that she made her presence known no matter her location. Lisa would talk shit to any nigga then tell him that he still better treat her like a Queen, or it would be problems for him and whoever else. Many women despised Lisa because of her attitude, but many women loved her and looked up to her because of her attitude. If a man was a sucker then Lisa wasn't the woman for him at all, but any real man knew she was a valuable woman to have by his side. Dunkin obviously didn't know the good things that came from being with a woman like Lisa, but he was about to see the bad.

"I know you niggas want to hear this song I'm trying to put together," said Lisa as she looked at all her goons.

Lisa had a full room sound proofed for her studio and that's where most of her time was spent. Her goal was to be better than any female rapper ever and she had the skills to be the best. She also had the money to push any album she wanted to put on the market. Lisa's only downfall was that she got a lot of her hope from wanting to prove other people wrong. The thing she didn't realize was that she didn't need to prove no one wrong because they really didn't give a fuck anyway.

"Hell yeah, you know we want to hear that Lunatic flow," answered one of her goons. Lisa then started to rap,

"Yo dick might go deep, but my throat go deeper.

Bad bitch all day, got em askin have you seen her.

Knockin bitches like I'm nun chuck, still ballin like I'm Taylor Chuck.

Fuck what these bitches talkin bout cuz honestly, I don't give a fuck.

I mix corruption with construction cuz I knock you, then I pick you up.

You can say what you want about me, but bitch I get them bands up.

Nigga asked could he marry me, I said not even when they bury me.

Nigga tried to get mad, so I called that nigga bear meat.

Fly high like a kite, major moves all night.

I ain't the one to fuck with, so you should say your prayers tonight." She then stopped to look at them.

"Damn, now that shit go hard right there. You going to make me get in that studio lil mama for real.

Cardy or Nikky are not I repeat are not ready for you. You rap like a straight nigga," said Tyler the goon who had just got done sucking her toes.

No Limit, which was one of her other goons was just sitting there looking at them like they were fools. To him the flows were lame he felt he could have done better, and he couldn't even rap. No Limit really wanted to kill the rest of the goons and be with Lisa by himself. He wanted to kill Dunkin on his own for Lisa and marry her afterwards. He was one of the types that didn't like peons or ass kissers. He didn't like the fact that Lisa let Tyler suck her toes. He was shitty that he didn't get to suck them this night, and it seemed like Tyler got to suck them every time. The only thought that ran through his mind was shooting Tyler in his head when he was on his knees sucking her toes. Then out of nowhere Tyler started to rap because Lisa left the beat going, he said,

"Hoe ass niggas check it up.

Bad bitches shake it up.

My name is big Tyler and I ain't never gave a fuck.

Got the gun to yo head bitch you out of fuckin luck.

I'm the chip you the hoy.

I'm a man you a boy.

You ain't ready this shit better tone ya shine up.

Nigga I'm running through this town all hooded and masked up.

You still thinking about breakfast, bitch I moved on to lunch." Then he was interrupted.

"Check this shit out y'all. This nigga in Jamaica right now," said Doo Doo as he showed all the others his iPhone with Dunkin going live in Jamaica.

Doo Doo was the biggest ass kisser of them all and always wanted to make Lisa think he was more on his game than the rest of the guy's.

Lisa snatched the phone out of his hands as he talked and said, "I just talked to his bitch ass sister Tyrea today and that bitch didn't say shit about him going to Jamaica. I wanted that son of a bitch dead tonight."

"Don't worry I hope his ass enjoys it because we going to make this his last trip," said No Limit.

"Something told me to look at my Facebook Lisa, you know I stay two steps ahead I really do this shit," said Doo Doo before he was interrupted.

"Nigga shut the fuck up you always sucking behind some ass nigga. You going to make me kill your ass I don't have time to hear that bullshit," said No Limit before he was also interrupted.

He seemed mad, but he was just hating on Doo Doo because he knew Lisa would give him brownie points.

"All you niggas shut the fuck up and get the fuck out my house. I want this nigga dead. I don't care if you motherfuckers have to go kill him in Jamaica, I want his bitch ass dead. And if I find out his bitch ass sister knew about him going and didn't mention it to me, I want that bitch dead too," said Lisa as she turned around to walk away after telling her pit bulls to watch the guys leave. Her dogs were somewhat like humans and understood every word she commanded.

Her goons turned around to leave. Once they got outside, they stood in a huddle to talk amongst each other. They all agreed that they wouldn't lay a finger on Tyrea no matter what Lisa said. They all knew that Tyrea was a sweet woman and she didn't have to tell Lisa nothing about Dunkin's trip. All of them knew Lisa used Tyrea as a spy and Tyrea had no idea she was being used. Their minds were made up that if Lisa would command them to do anything to Tyrea, they would have to kill Lisa right then and there. They knew Lisa was scandalous, and they couldn't go for killing Tyrea because they all grew up with her. Though Lisa was the woman of all their dreams they couldn't let her influence them to do nothing to an innocent woman. They all had grown up with Dunkin too, but his life wasn't as important to them as his sister's life. Dunkin had caused all of them pain, so they didn't give a fuck about killing him by a long shot.

Meanwhile, Dunkin was in Jamaica having the time of his life. After getting off his flight and going to his other girlfriend's beach house in Kingston, all he wanted to do was lay on the beach. As he laid on the beach, he smoked some of the best weed Jamaica had to offer.

"Where my viewers at on this bitch," asked Dunkin as he stared into the camera of his iPhone talking to Facebook?

He was laid back on the sand on his Louis Vuitton cover, smoking an extended joint, with snacks all around. After he was up to four hundred viewers he started to talk,

"I can see clear through this Louie frames. How you motherfuckers what in Indianapolis? I than got all the way to Kingston and still can only think about a Gyro combo from Jordan's Fish and Chicken. Guess I'm a just settle for some jerk chicken from here, but I'll be to see you Jordan's as soon as I get home. I can't say when I'll be back though. I'm a get this sun in my life for the time being," said Dunkin as he put his two long braids over his shoulders and hit his joint as he laid back.

Lisa was on a fake page while laying naked in her bed foaming in the mouth. She was mad and could only think of the day that she would finally kill Dunkin or have him killed. She couldn't help but to feel on her perky breast and play with her clit while looking at his live video on Facebook though. She thought the baby in her stomach would make her and Dunkin be together forever. She couldn't get that, but knew that once Dunkin was dead, she would at least get a portion of his estate. Lisa knew that Dunkin had something put away for all his children. She figured she deserved something from him after he played her the way he did.

"Well let me get up out of here Facebook I got business to take care of. Let a boss do some boss shit," said Dunkin as multiple women begged him not to go as he turned off his camera.

After the video was over Lisa jumped to her feet. She stood in front of her body length mirror looking at her perfectly shaped naked body. As tears rolled down her face she said, "How could your bitch ass leave me, and I started to love you? How could you leave me with a child and not want us to be a family? How could you lie to me and tell me you loved me, but leave me on the curb like trash?"

She stood there looking at the mirror for about sixty more seconds without saying a word to herself and out of nowhere, she said, "bitch I'm a see to it that I burn your punk ass alive."

She looked into her own eyes through the mirror and all you could see was murder. After that she laid back down and thought about what she could have done wrong to Dunkin. As she thought about how she put her all into sucking his dick and learned new ways to ride his dick she got madder and madder. Then she thought about Milly and how much better she looked than Milly and got even madder. She then picked up the phone to call Tyrea.

"Girl you didn't tell me your brother was going to Jamaica. That boy knows he be getting up out of Nap Town," said Lisa as she chuckled talking to Dunkin's sister Tyrea.

"You know I don't talk to that boy like that I didn't even know. How you doing though? You trying to go to Wing Stop and get some of them Lemon Pepper wings later," asked Tyrea as she looked at her clock and seen it was three in the morning?

"You know it baby, shoot I wish they were opened now," said Lisa as she laughed.

"Okay girl let me get a few more hours of sleep. Do you need me to come over? Are you okay? Don't be letting nothing stress you out, you got my nephew in your stomach," replied Tyrea.

"Yeah, I'm okay, I guess. Just was up and thinking about you. You know I'm up more when it's dark outside. Get you some sleep though I'll call you around ten," said Lisa.

"Okay, I'll come get you when you're ready. Quit that stressing girl," said Tyrea as she disconnected the call.

While Lisa had a rock-solid plan to kill Dunkin, she just didn't know she was in line to get the honor to do so because there was plenty of others planning to do the same thing. Not only were rival drug dealers calculating plans to end his life due to his drug empire, but other heartbroken women were on the prowl for him too. While Dunkin had everyone fearing him, he just didn't know that he was too comfortable in the game. I guess after going untouched so long in the game anyone would get comfortable. Fear doesn't stay in people's heart for long though especially a heartbroken woman.

There was a tatted up white girl named Passion who worked at a strip club called PT's. Dunkin had been having fun with her for years. She felt she should have been number one in his life and never wanted to let go of him. Dunkin had met her one night and liked her because he couldn't fuck her the same night. Passion was a good girl gone bad. She started off as a medical assistant and went on to become the director of the same hospital where she started. Passion just couldn't give up snorting cocaine after her ex-husband turned her out on the drug. Then once she left her ex-husband due to him always cheating, he called and told the hospital to drug test her, once they did, they found cocaine in her system. After going on administrative leave for over a month then she was fired. Once she exhausted all her funds, she went into the stripping industry. Her career change wasn't a surprise to many because she had the body of a goddess.

"What's up with you," asked Dunkin as he approached Passion the night, he met her?

"Nothing, do you want a dance or something," asked Passion as she entertained Dunkin only thinking about business and nothing personal? At that time in her life she wasn't looking for a man she only wanted money.

"Shit, you the coldest bitch in her tonight I don't see why I wouldn't," answered Dunkin as he pulled a stack of ones out his pocket.

Within seconds Passion was grinding on Dunkin's lap to the sounds of Trey Song's "I need a girl" song. While she didn't know or care to know who Dunkin was, every other dancer knew exactly who he was, and they wanted Dunkin to fuck. Passion was used to getting her own money so nothing about money would make her look twice. Her only mission was to get money and she figured since she was only thirty-three, she could still have another chance in the medical field. All she wanted to do was dance for the time being and then move to North Carolina. After moving to North Carolina, she planned to do what she loved to do which was take care of patients.

Dunkin made it rain on Passion all night and bought her shot after shot of Patron. Passion killed every song so much that even Dunkin's crew made it rain on her as well. When Dunkin slipped his dick out his pants Passion didn't have a clue as the strobe lights made it hard for anyone to see. She didn't have the slightest idea of what he was doing. She was so drunk that once she sat her bare ass on his lap again and felt his dick on her she just continued to grind on him and let it go between her butt cheeks. Dunkin was able to get the head of his dick in Passion's pussy, but after the head was in, she stopped him. She turned around and smiled at him before snatching her money up and leaving. After that Dunkin made his mind up that he had to fuck Passion.

After the night ended, Dunkin told his crew that he was going to stay back. They didn't like the fact that he wanted to stay back because they knew he had been drinking and looked like a walking lick. Though he was well known they knew it only took a thirsty broke nigga to see him out and have their way with him. Dunkin had on an all gold Balmain short outfit, with the new gold and white Jordan's on to match. He was draping in jewelry with a fifteen-thousand-dollar Cuban link necklace on, a Rolex watch, golf ball size diamond earrings in his ears and a diamond ring on each index finger. And like any other time, he had his two corn rolls coming down and hanging over the front of his shoulders. He sat out in the parking lot in his brand new

2014 Stingray Corvette waiting for Passion to come out of the club.

CHAPTER 3

"Hey, now you know I been waiting an hour out here for you. Why don't we head to Denny's for breakfast and get to know each other a little better," asked Dunkin as he approached Passion while leaving the music bumping in his Corvette? All you could hear was Yo Gotti's song, "Cold game" booming from his sound system.

"I don't go out with strangers and I could have fucking smacked you for putting your dick inside me. You went too far dude," replied Passion.

The other dancers were in their cars watching the whole interaction between Passion and Dunkin. The other women wished they were in Passion's position at this time. Passion had got scared when Dunkin put his dick in her that's why she left his presence so fast. It didn't feel bad to her, but she felt violated like he raped her for doing such a bold act without her consent.

"Baby girl, as a man I apologize for that and I normally don't do shit like that, but I started thinking of a name for our baby as soon as I laid eyes on you," said Dunkin.

For some reason what he said made Passion smile. She wasn't used to a line like Dunkin had just put on her. Shit she was from Martinsville, Indiana where it was primarily white people and they were all lame. She had never dated a thug in her life, let alone anything with African American blood in their body. Her family was very prejudice and made sure they kept her away from black people growing up because her father knew she had a body a black man would love. Though as she got older, she started to sneak off and listen to black people music and eventually had a female best friend who was black. She still wasn't used to the swag of a black man but so far, she liked it.

"Well that's nice to know, but I don't go out with strangers. Maybe come here and see me a few more times and we can talk about a date then. Sorry, but that's just how I am," said Passion.

"That's cool I respect that. All yeah and you forgot something when you tried to snatch your money up all fast after I pulled that bullshit in the club," said Dunkin as he pulled five one hundred dollar bills out his pocket and handed them to Passion.

"Wow are you serious," asked Passion as she grabbed the money out of his hand with no hesitation?

"Yeah, I wanted you to have a good night with your tips. For some reason you don't seem like you should even be dancing. I see a lot of strippers and you just don't seem like the type, so I wanted you to have a good night," said Dunkin as he looked Passion in her blue eyes.

"Well, I surely need it. I can't begin to thank you enough. Give me your phone you seem like a cool guy," said Passion as she took the iPhone that Dunkin handed her. She dialed her number from his phone and let her phone ring so they would have each other's phone number.

"I'll be in contact with you beautiful," said Dunkin as he turned to walk away. Really, he was shitty because he wanted to fuck right then and there.

"And don't be walking around sticking your dick in everything so easily. That's totally not a good look dude there is too many diseases going around out here. I used to work in the medical field, so I've seen many different situations," said Passion as she stopped Dunkin before he walked away.

"Right on baby girl I guess I did get beside myself. I don't normally do shit like that. Usually I got that Magnum XL on super tight," said Dunkin.

"Yeah I guess you do need an XL," said Passion as she chuckled and walked to her 2010 Nissan Maxima.

Passion pulled off, but before Dunkin could pull off two strippers that knew who he was tried to stop him and offer him Denny's. Dunkin told them he was good and headed home to Milly for the rest of the night. For some reason he liked Passion. He was a person who never had feelings for a woman he just met and sometimes he wouldn't have feelings even if he knew them for years. In his mind though he wasn't going to get his feelings caught up with no bitch. Dunkin was still trying to love Milly and they weren't far from their date to get married. Milly was the type of woman any man could love, but Dunkin found it hard to do. She was beautiful, intelligent, and had a good heart. On top of that Milly didn't need anyone's money. Her family was very wealthy and ever since she had been fourteen, she owned her own sewing business. Through her sewing business she had already made enough money to be set for life. She was also looking into fashion designing, which was off to a good start and hadn't even started yet.

After Dunkin eventually broke Passion's heart she was never the same again. She started snorting cocaine and selling her body to support her habit. Her family tried sending her to rehabilitation, but every time she went, she would escape again. Her father, nor the rest of her family knew what was going on in her life. She went from being an executive type woman to a coke head hooker and her daughter didn't see her for weeks at a time. When it would seem like she was getting her head back together she would drift off again just by the thought of Dunkin. She fell in love with Dunkin and though Dunkin did fall for her he just couldn't let his heart get involved with Passion. Then the day came that she finally talked to her mother about what she was going through.

"Mom I don't fucking care anymore. I want to die, please take care of my daughter," said Passion.

"Heather, you have to tell me what's going on. I can't see you like this; you have a family that loves you," said her mother as she called Passion by her real name. None of her family even knew she stripped so her stage name Passion didn't even exist to them.

"There's a guy I met by the name of Dunkin. I'm still in love with him, but he treats me like shit, and I hate myself because maybe it's something I did to make him feel this way about me," said Passion.

"You've never told me or your dad about a man you were dating. When did this come about? Where did he come from? Who is he," asked her mother?

"He's from Indianapolis and I've never told you guys about him because he's half black, but I love him. Dunkin has once loved me too," said Passion as she sat there looking like she was half human and half crackhead.

"Heather you have to be fucking kidding me. You're a fucking nigger lover. You're a disgrace to this family and we don't accept you anymore. We will take full custody of your daughter because we can't have her grow up and be a nigger lover like you. Just wait until I tell your dad," said her mother.

As Passion was getting up to leave her mother grabbed her by the arm and pulled her back. Passion knew her mother was about to take the matter to her dad, but it was what she expected. Passion's father was the president of the Aryan brotherhood from his area. He had been in and out of prison and found a name for himself with the brotherhood. He was a big ass white dude with a bald head. Tattoos covered his body and he had a swastika tattooed on the back of his bald head. In prison he wasn't a joke, and neither was he on the streets. One thing everyone knew was that he loved his daughter with all his heart. He wasn't just going around disrespecting black people, but in his heart, he believed the white race shouldn't be mixed with no race especially the black race. He came from Martinsville after all. A town that blacks pretty much weren't allowed in and if they were there, they were usually selling dope and would immediately get caught. Just because they were black the judge usually gave them as much as fifty years for something as simple as a twenty piece.

"Talk to your fucking daughter. She's in love with a fucking nigger," said Passions mother as she walked away and left Passion with her father.

"With a fucking nigger? What the hell Heather, I've taught you better than that. You know them people are nothing but the devil. Is this why you've let yourself go like this my dear? I'm going to bury that nigger I promise," said Big Sam, Passions father.

Passion's mother was mad when Big Sam didn't smack the shit out of his daughter like he did her when he found out she let two black men fuck her at the same time. She had stayed away from Big Sam for over three weeks' when she ran off with the two black men. She fell in love so much with black dick that she considered stealing her and Big Sam's lifesavings and moving to

Florida. She wanted both black men to move with her to Florida. They ran so many trains on her that Big Sam couldn't have sex with her for two months because her pussy was so swollen. He had to take her to the emergency room to get medical treatment because her pussy was so swollen and her nipple's as well. Her nipples were swollen because she liked them sucked hard and both men had a titty each to suck all day. Big Sam ended up forgiving her but always kept the situation a secret. He kept it a secret because he didn't want to be embarrassed by his family and friends.

"Dad I'm sorry," said Passion as she broke down crying. Her father held her letting her know that he was still on her side.

"I want her out of my fucking house," said Passion's mother as she stormed back into the living room. She was mad because she always felt like Big Sam had their daughters back more than he had her back. He had smacked the shit out of her as soon as she came back in the door from being with the two black men, but now he was just holding his daughter like a baby.

"You sit down right now slutty bitch. You've ran off with two big black dicks' before you bitch. So big that I had to take you to the hospital because your pussy was so swollen. Yeah, you never told Heather that, so get the hell out of here. I'm going to see to it that I kill the nigger dead that hurt my daughter," said Big Sam. Passion was surprised to hear about her mother running off with black men.

"I hate you, you're nothing but a white bastard. I'm going to run to some black dick now you fucker," said Heather's mother as tears rolled down her face and she ran out the door.

"Now tell me everything you know about this nigger. I'm going to hang him by his toes. No one does my baby girl wrong," said Big Sam.

"His name is Dunkin, he's from Indianapolis and he's very dangerous. He's very rich as well. I don't think you can beat him dad," said Passion as she tried to lay her head on her father's chest.

"You never say a nigger can beat me bitch," said Big Sam as he started to choke his daughter. This was the first time he ever raised a hand to Passion. After a few seconds he released her and started to cry himself.

"I'm sorry dad, but I don't know what to fucking do," said Passion as she continued to cry.

"It's okay I have all the information I need. I have a black guy I know from prison who is known in the Indy area I'm going to give him a call to find Mr. Dunkin. I just have to find my guy now; his name is Eric I just can't remember his number," said Big Sam.

While in prison Big Sam met a black guy by the name of Eric, who he got very close to and respected to the fullest. Though Big Sam was an Aryan and Eric was with the Moorish Science Temple of America they found a connection with each and always remained friends. The thing that Big Sam didn't know was that Eric was Dunkin's personal trainer. Eric didn't have a public Facebook page so Big Sam would have to dig deep to find Eric. Big Sam and Eric always did favors for each other while in prison, so he needed to find Eric. From that day forward Dunkin had another enemy he had no idea about.

Lisa and Tyrea were sitting at Wing Stop eating their wings and fries. Tyrea would cheat on her diet here and there just to eat some lemon pepper wings. Ever since Lisa had turned her onto Wing Stop, she had been addicted. Being that she was a healthy eater she felt she deserved to eat some wings every now and then. Eric was her trainer as well as being Dunkin's personal trainer. Eric told her that he cheated every now and again on his diet too, but he didn't make it a habit. Eric had told Tyrea not to make it a habit as well, but she didn't listen. Tyrea had picked Lisa up from her house and treated her to wings that day. When they went out together, they were both so beautiful that they usually had to turn men away from paying their bills from wherever they went to eat or shop. Every now and again someone would pay their bills without them knowing it was coming until they tried to pay.

"You know I don't like my brother, but he's still my brother and I don't want to be talking about him in a bad way or talk about any of his business to anyone. You my girl and I love you to death, I'm not your friend just because you used to date my brother and have my nephew in your stomach," said Tyrea as she looked Lisa in the eyes.

"Tyrea, I know that, why are you telling me that," asked Lisa?

"Nothing big, it was just weird that you called me at three in the morning asking me why I didn't tell you my brother was going to Jamaica," replied Tyrea.

"Girl that wasn't nothing like that. I had just seen him live on Facebook and was really surprised. It was more less a joke," said Lisa as she tried to play it off and giggle. Really inside she wanted to slap the shit out of Tyrea.

"You are too silly lady," said Tyrea as she laughed back at Lisa.

CHAPTER 4

Abayomi and Dunkin were out enjoying each other's company. They never really got to spend time with each other, so they were enjoying every second of one another. No one knew that Dunkin had built a lot of things in Jamaica with Abayomi. On this trip Dunkin was starting to do something that he had never really done in life and that was fall in love. The meaning of Abayomi's name was the "bringer of happiness" and that was what she brought to Dunkin's life, true peace. Dunkin had no intentions of leaving Milly, but he never had plans to leave Abayomi neither. Sometimes he would just say what Abayomi wanted to hear. He knew in his heart that if it wasn't for Milly, he would have been living right in Jamaica with Abayomi with no worries. For the time being he figured he would just live his best life and say fuck who had a problem with it.

They ended up going to eat at Jade Garden Restaurant which was high end Chinese food. Dunkin liked spicy food, so he ordered Chicken in Black Bean Sauce. Abayomi ordered Sweet and Spicy Chicken Wings with fried rice. Jade Garden Restaurant was one of the best Chinese food restaurants in Kingston. Dunkin only took Abayomi to the best places whenever he was in her presence. Dunkin had already taken her to the mall and spent over seventeen thousand dollars buying her things she didn't even need. Though she didn't want or need him to, he still liked to shower her with gifts. Buying her things, she would probably never get to wear because her wardrobe was already too much for her to handle.

When they got back to Abayomi's beach house Dunkin sat back on the couch and turned on the Cleveland and Houston basketball game. He stripped down to his boxers when he got in the door. Abayomi went in her room so she wouldn't disturb him watching his game. She stripped down as well. Her caramel skin looked good enough to eat. Though she wasn't thick like most of the women Dunkin had been with she still had a shape that was better than all of them. Her pretty face should have been on the front of a magazine. She had caramel skin and around her nipples was just a little bit darker.

Dunkin was in Jamaica with NuNu when he met Abayomi. He did everything in his power to get away from NuNu so he could introduce himself to her like a gentleman. Once he did get her attention, he didn't leave her attention, by force. He left NuNu at the bar by herself in Kingston for hours, while he walked all around Kingston getting to know Abayomi. That night Dunkin was casually dressed in a white and black Burberry short sleeve shirt with a red collar and white Balmain shorts. He only wore a three-carat diamond ring for jewelry and had on all white Burberry London Check and Leather sneakers. None of that impressed

Abayomi though, what impressed her was that he never gave up. They walked and talked for hours before he went back to the bar with NuNu.

When Dunkin walked Abayomi home, she told him Kingston wasn't the place for him to be walking around alone. He showed her the gun he had on him and told her he wasn't worried. She wondered how he got the gun considering it was hard for Americans to get them there, but she just let it go. She came from a family of gangsters, so she liked it really. Once Dunkin got back to the bar, he seen Jamaican men surrounding NuNu laughing and talking with her like they were having a good time. Dunkin got jealous immediately. He didn't hesitate to let them know she was his woman. NuNu didn't want to hear him though, she smacked the taste buds out his mouth.

"So, you ready for your dessert daddy," said Abayomi as she moved her naked body closer to Dunkin.

Dunkin sat there and just stared at her beautiful body. At that time, he knew he wanted to be with her every day for the rest of his life. He didn't care anymore, and he was now knowing what his father meant when he told him about truly loving one woman. Abayomi was everything he could ask for in a woman and though Milly had her own money too, she didn't have a beautiful personality like Abayomi did. Dunkin was ready to propose to her and he really wanted to be her husband. He figured he would marry Milly in the United States and marry her in Jamaica. Then just keep things the way they had been with him traveling back and forth. In his heart he felt he couldn't let go of Milly or Abayomi.

"Back that ass up to my face baby," said Dunkin as he looked seductively into Abayomi's eyes.

She did what he said and started to back up as he sat on the couch looking like a kid waiting on a snack cake. When she got her ass backed up to his face enough, he spread her butt cheek apart and started to massage her asshole with his chin before his tongue entered it. At the same time, he was playing with her clit using his fingers. After just three minutes she was started to squirt while standing up. It poured out of her like a faucet. That's when Dunkin got on his knee's from sitting on the couch and started to lick her juices from off her toes first before moving up and eating her pussy. He did all this while she was still standing up.

As she moaned, she said with her lovely accent, "It's my turn to please you daddy, that's all I want to do is please you forever."

"I'm more than pleased sweetie, now let me get back to my basketball game," said Dunkin as he looked at the woman of his dreams while wiping his face.

"You are so boring Dunkin; I want to suck your dick tonight," said Abayomi.

"Baby, sometimes I just want to please you without getting pleased in return. I love you. Now go and get some sleep," said Dunkin.

"I wouldn't have a world without you. I love you so much," said Abayomi as she walked away with her ass bouncing left to right. Though her ass wasn't big like most women she was still the shit.

Dunkin sat back down and started to watch the game again. He eventually got up and walked to the stereo to turn on some light music. He turned on one of his favorite slow songs by New Edition, "Can you stand the rain." After a few minutes he turned the game off and laid back to meditate. Dunkin had a lot on his mind and wanted to make his next move his best move. Any other man would have been happy to be in his situation or so they thought, but he was looking for something different in life. He knew that if Dizzy was still living, he would be right in Jamaica with him. Dizzy had a side piece a few beach houses down who used to love him to death as well. Dunkin felt it was time to man up and just be with two women, leaving the rest of the many women he had with broken hearts.

After listening to music and meditating for a while Dunkin decided to get up and go to the kitchen to wash the few dishes that were in the sink. Abayomi didn't like him washing dishes, but that was something Dunkin was immune to doing. Milly always told him he didn't have to do so many chores around the house as well, Dunkin liked things a certain way though. Whatever clothes he didn't send to the cleaners, he washed on his own. Dunkin liked his things to be a certain way and didn't mind doing it himself to make sure things were done the way he liked it. Those habits in Dunkin were taught to him by his parents.

Back in Indianapolis, Zynika, Terrance, and Draco were sitting in the stash house counting money and measuring up dope. Nicole had gone out to the gas station to grab more Swishers. Dunkin hadn't been gone long and the crew had already racked in over two hundred thousand dollars. They were so used to counting large quantities of money that it didn't mean nothing to them. Many people's eyes would have been big and been excited counting that much money, but they counted the money like they were tired of it.

Nicole left the gas station and was headed back to the stash house. She grabbed ten packs of Diamond Swisher's, five one-dollar bags of fruity Tootsie Rolls, and four thirty-two-ounce Body Armor drinks banana strawberry flavored. Only thing on her mind was rolling up a blunt and smoking. She won a bet with the rest of the crew, so she didn't have to count no money or weigh up no dope for the night. She still wanted to be at the house just in case Dunkin did pull one of his surprise appearances like he usually did. Nicole was cruising in her 750 LI BMW she had just purchased. Everybody in Dunkin's crew rolled big.

"Get the fuck down," said the men masked up in Ku Klux Klan costumes as they bum rushed Dunkin's stash house. All you seen was assault rifles and handguns with beams on them coming in the door. They came in so quick that no one had a chance to react. All they could do was what the men told them or either get killed.

"Man, what the fuck, I'm not getting on no fucking floor. Fuck you motherfuckers," said Draco. Draco was never the type to fear nothing and no one.

"I guess you tough huh, Draco I will kill you fucking dead. All you motherfuckers are lucky this ambush isn't meant for you bitches. We don't want that punk ass money or dope that's on the table neither," said one of the masked men.

"Then what the fuck do you bitch ass motherfuckers want then. We all trained to go and if that means go to the grave then we ready for that too," said Zynika. She was trying to make out the voices of the robbers like the rest of the crew was doing. The men all had voice converters made into their gowns so that was impossible to do.

"Bitch you shut your thick ass up. Robbery or murder wasn't in the plan today but that don't mean the shit can't happen. I'd probably want to rape your pretty ass too, so don't tempt me. This mission is a mission of showing your bitch ass boss Dunkin that we are on his ass. His days are numbered out here. You tell that half breed when he comes from Jamaica that he better stay the fuck out of dodge," said one of the masked men as they all made their way back out the house.

"What the fuck," said Draco as he tried to get up while the men were leaving. Before he could even get his body off the ground, he was shot dead by one of the masked men.

"I told you motherfuckers to stay the fuck down. That was the example, don't make me have to make all you motherfucker's examples. Don't nobody get up until we are out the fucking house," said one of the other masked men as he simultaneously put the red beam on all of their heads.

After the men left the house Terrance, Zynika, and Nicole all started to shed tears. What made the situation even worst for Nicole is that Draco was her brother. She didn't know how she would explain things to her mother. Nicole stood about five foot four with some nice measurements and a pretty face. She used to deal with Dunkin and that's how Draco and Dunkin were introduced. Now Nicole was feeling like it was her fault for her brother dying.

"Noooooooooo," said Nicole as she was on her knees over her brothers' dead body.

"I am totally lost for words," said Zynika as she sat there crying with Nicole.

Terrance was getting all the money and drugs out the house before the police arrived. In his mind he knew there was about to be a war. The only problem he could see with going to war was that he didn't know who they were going to war with. He knew whoever had come in the house was trained and professional. They had no clue who the men were in the Ku Klux Klan gowns and on top of that they had voice boxes. They dreaded telling Dunkin what happened knowing his reaction was going to be to go to war with everyone in the city who he felt had a problem.

NuNu was sitting back talking to her mother Georgia. She was very upset about Dunkin not giving her the attention he had always given. Though they had been split up for years, Dunkin would still go through her house to lay up with her, but that hadn't been happening and she didn't like it. NuNu knew about Milly's pregnancy only because one of her cousin's worked at the hospital Milly went to. Her cousin seen Milly in the hospital and heard her talking to the doctor. Milly told the doctor she didn't want the child's father to know until a later time. NuNu knew how Dunkin was about having kids and that the news would excite him. The thing was that NuNu had been his only baby momma for years and didn't want to share her position.

NuNu knew everything about Dunkin and figured she would use it to her advantage. It wasn't even a week earlier when she called her cousins from Chicago. She told them she had a mission for them to complete. Her whole family were Gangster Disciples out of Chicago who weren't for no games when it came to their family. NuNu didn't tell them the real reason she wanted Lisa and Milly dead, but she did make it clear to her cousins that she wanted the women dead. She tried to keep Dunkin out the conversation but couldn't, her cousins made it known to her that they wanted to rob Dunkin and had been wanting to for years. The thought of something happening to Dunkin didn't sit well with NuNu at all. She figured she would play it off with them so they would kill Lisa and Milly. Once that was done, she planned to have a meeting with her cousins and kill them before they could touch Dunkin. After all that was done, she felt in her heart Dunkin would run to her and they would live happily ever after.

Seemed like while NuNu was having meetings with her cousins, Lisa was also doing the same thing with her crew. Lisa had pulled Doo Doo and Tyler to a secret meeting without none of the other men in her crew. She told them that she wanted to start applying pressure immediately to Dunkin and his family. The thing Doo Doo and Tyler didn't agree with was the fact that she told them she wanted Dunkin's sister Tyrea raped and killed. In both of their minds they knew Lisa needed to be killed herself, but they both were too in love with her to kill her themselves. The thing they both knew is that if it came down to a situation where it was either Tyrea gets killed or Lisa, they would have to kill Lisa. Their plan was to apply pressure in every other direction, but to stay away from Tyrea.

Milly had just gotten back home and let her and Dunkin's female Kita out the house. This dog's name was Rossie. They both loved the dog to death. Though they had other dogs Rossie was in the house by herself because she was in heat. Milly had just gotten back from seeing Dunkin's parents and his sister Tyrea. She told them that she was pregnant and didn't know how to tell Dunkin. Deacon told her that she better make sure she tell Dunkin immediately. He knew it would make Dunkin mad if she held a secret like that for too long. The embrace Milly got from Dunkin's family was more than she ever expected and made her feel like she was finally part of the family. After all the time she had been with Dunkin she felt like an outsider to his family, now she finally had what she wanted. They laughed and talked for hours before Milly decided to go home.

As Milly waited for her toast to be done, she heard a loud sound coming from the upstairs part of the house. After that she heard the dog running to the door, but instead of the dog barking she was crying. Milly ran to the door to open it for the only protection she felt she had. Their house was so ducked off that she never thought there would be a problem in their home. From the sound and look of things she knew she was in for trouble though. When she opened the door all the cocaine white fur that usually covered their dog was now covered in dirt. There were also some words written in all black marker on the dog's fur. The words read, "Dunkin you're a dead man."

Just as Milly started to realize what was going on, she turned around, and she was hit in the head by an object so fast that her last thought left her mind. She hit the ground and blood started to pour all over her all white Gucci robe. Things happened so fast that she wasn't prepared in no way for what had just happened to her. In all the years of her life she had never been in so much pain. There was nothing she could do but lay there like she was paralyzed.

CHAPTER 5

Dunkin was washing dishes with wireless Beats earphones on his ears listening to slow jams. He glanced down at his Apple watch and seen the words emergency on it. He dried his hands off and grabbed his phone off the counter. For some reason he felt on edge, but in his mind, he was untouchable. The thought of someone doing something to him, his family, or his click never crossed his mind. He went where Abayomi couldn't hear him and made a call to Zynika.

"It's all bad, Dunkin," said Zynika as she cried into the phone. For some reason Dunkin had always been the one who made Zynika feel safe, but with what had just happened she didn't feel so safe anymore.

"Zynika, calm the fuck down and tell me what the fuck is going on. I'm about to be on my way back," said Dunkin though his plans were to be in Jamaica for another two weeks.

"Some people in Ku Klux Klan gowns came in the house and killed Draco. You need to hurry and get back this is too much to talk about over the phone," said Zynika still crying between every word.

"Say no more," said Dunkin as he hung up the phone. He squeezed his phone so hard after he hung up that it bent some.

Dunkin went into Abayomi's room and just stared at her from the door. From the look on his face she knew something was wrong with him. She got up and walked to the doorway to hold him not knowing what was going on she just wanted to comfort him. Though Dunkin wanted to make love to her one more time before leaving he didn't have the energy to. He knew in his heart that he needed to be back in Indianapolis immediately and would never let his crew down. In all his years of knowing Zynika he had never known her to cry. Even after people in her family had died, he never seen her shed a tear, so he knew something serious was going on and he had to be there for his people.

"Baby, I have to get back to the states. One of my homies just got killed and I don't know what's going on. I'll be back once I get everything under control, sorry baby," said Dunkin as he looked into the sad watery eyes of the woman he loved.

"No need for sorry honey. I know how it is being you. Well I don't know, but I could just imagine. I need to be in Australia for some business anyway. You know I love you and if you need me just give me a call," said Abayomi as she hugged and kissed Dunkin.

Back in Indianapolis, Lisa was scrolling Facebook when she seen a news update from Fox 59, which was a local news station. She seen a house that was too familiar to her eyes. It was the house that she most recently found out was Dunkin's stash house. She seen Draco's name come across the screen and was lost for words. The caption read, "there was one homicide in an apparent home invasion, the next to kin has been contacted. The deceased man's name is Tony Plotts." Lisa couldn't believe what she was reading. She knew for a fact she hadn't plotted anything on the house, so now her mind was wondering. Her main concern was getting to Nicole because she knew how close Nicole was to her brother. And though they were a part of Dunkin's crew she still had nothing but respect for them. It was Nicole and Draco that helped her whenever she needed money or anything else, she needed.

NuNu was at her house watching the news like she did every morning while drinking her coffee. Though she still had a thing for Dunkin she still had to have her needs met on a daily. Her fling Fat Boy was laying in her bed while she was out in the kitchen doing her daily morning duties. That's when she seen what she also knew was a familiar house to her, it was Dunkin's stash house. The news took NuNu by surprise just like it did Lisa. After all, NuNu was very close to Draco and Nicole, so when she seen that it was Draco who was killed, she couldn't do nothing, but cry. NuNu never considered Draco a snitch, but she did get information about Dunkin from him whenever she wanted. The information was more friendly than anything. She could hear Draco in her mind then telling her that she knew Dunkin was going to come back to her so she should quit stressing. And though NuNu never needed anything Draco would still look out for her especially when she hooked him up with her female friends. NuNu tried to call Nicole, but as she expected there was no answer.

"My nigga get your shit on and get out my house," said NuNu as she talked to Fat Boy. NuNu stood there looking like an African goddess. She stood five foot eight and had the body that many women spent thousands of dollars to have.

"Let me get some sleep. You crazy as fuck. Have me eating your pussy all night, licking your ass, and sucking your toes and think I'm not going to be tired," replied Fat Boy as he went back to sleep like she never said a word to him.

"So, you're complaining," said NuNu as she crawled from the bottom of the bed up to Fat Boy and started to give him some head.

No matter what NuNu loved her some Fat Boy and one of the main reasons she loved him was because he wasn't scared of Dunkin. She had dated a few other men, but none of them wanted Dunkin to know she was dating them. Fat Boy was one of them nigga's that just didn't give a fuck because he loved NuNu that much. He was willing to put his life on the line for NuNu and her children because he knew they were part of her. Whenever NuNu sucked his dick she gave him treatment that she had only given to Dunkin.

"Shit baby, now you know I can't get up now," said Fat Boy as his body tensed up.

"Get some sleep. I'm heading over to Dunkin's stash house. I just seen that Draco got killed last night over there and want to go support Nicole," said NuNu.

"Man, what the fuck. I just bought four bricks from him last night. When did this shit happen," asked Fat Boy? Another thing NuNu liked about Fat Boy was that he had a heart and he was all about his money. She just never knew why she always kept him a secret thinking that one day her and Dunkin would be back together.

"Get you some sleep. I'll tell you everything later after I talk to Nicole. I know she is an emotional wreck right now. I'll be back in a few hours baby. I'll order you some Denny's through DoorDash since I won't be here to make you breakfast," said NuNu after she slipped on her Nike leggings, Nike tank top, and her Air Max 95's ready to head out the door.

NuNu got to Dunkin's stash house. She was surprised to see Lisa standing there, but she wasn't going to start an argument under the circumstances that were at hand. She went to Nicole and hugged her very tight. For some reason the tears had stopped falling from Nicole's face and she went numb. Draco was all she really had in the world. No kids, one parent, no other siblings. Nicole grabbed NuNu by the hand and lead her back to a room where they could be alone. Lisa felt some type of way about them going away in private but didn't let her facial expression show her feelings.

"Whoever is responsible for this, I want them dead NuNu and I want to kill them myself," said Nicole as she started to cry again because she couldn't hold back her tears anymore.

"Baby, I know how you feel, but I don't want you thinking like that right now. Let me figure this out and I promise we will take care of the situation," said NuNu as she looked into Nicole's teary eyes.

NuNu couldn't do nothing but feel bad for Nicole. She had never heard Nicole mention killing anyone, so she knew when Nicole said it her heart had to have been broken. The only thought on NuNu's mind was that Dunkin had a lot of secret enemies. With him having so many secret enemies they probably would never find out who had killed Draco or maybe even had it done. NuNu wasn't going to let that stop her from trying to figure out who was behind it though. In her heart she knew just like Nicole knew that Dunkin would be emotionless. That was one thing upon many other things that people didn't like about Dunkin. NuNu's suspicions grew even more at the fact that no drugs or money was taken. After NuNu heard nothing was taken from Nicole her mind began to wonder. The news let NuNu know that somebody was out to get Dunkin in the same manner she was trying to get him. The cold truth was that she knew it was another woman in love with him who was behind the attack. She doubted Lisa because she felt Lisa was too soft to even get in a fight with anyone.

NuNu went and said bye to everyone in the house including Lisa before walking out the house in rage. The fact that someone had killed Draco didn't set well on NuNu's brain. She couldn't believe the number of lives that had been lost from people dealing with Dunkin. She still couldn't get over the fact that Dizzy had lost his life dealing with Dunkin as well. In her heart she knew if someone ran up on Dunkin's mother porch to rob someone it would have had to been Dunkin they were trying to rob. It was a lot she was trying to figure out at the time. As NuNu pulled off her phone started to ring.

"Mommy, please come get us out this house. Some people put guns to us telling us they are going to kill daddy and wanted us to give him the message," said Tamara. Which was Dunkin's and NuNu's daughter.

"Where are you at baby? Oh my God, are you okay," asked NuNu as her voice started to crack?

"We are at Dexter's house. We are fine, we just can't get out the house. They put boards up to all the windows from the outside and we don't know what they used to keep them in place. Dexter and DJ have been kicking the boards, but they won't come off. They took our phones, but Dexter had a spare phone in the house that we had to find in the dark because they cut all the power to the house. Mommy I'm scared please come here now. We have been in here since last night," said Tamara.

"Baby stay on the phone with me I'm on the way there right now," said NuNu. She had to stay strong for her baby's, she knew if her daughter heard her cry it would make her cry as well. So, she held her tears in and pondered on the thought that it was time for war. The only thing on her mind now was getting to her children and then getting in touch with Dunkin.

Dunkin had just gotten to the airport in Jamaica. He tried to be out of Jamaica way sooner, but no flights were going out of the country when he started requesting flights. The only thing on his mind was murder, he couldn't believe someone had balls enough to go in one of his houses. His intentions was to get back to Indianapolis and turn the whole city on fire. Draco's life did mean something to him, but he was mainly mad because someone had enough balls to go in one of his houses. Out of all his years in the game no one had ever tested him in this type of way. Whoever it was Dunkin planned to make an example out of them.

Meanwhile, Lisa had left from Dunkin's stash house and was meeting up with Tyler and Doo Doo. She had a thousand questions to ask them. She just knew they weren't the ones responsible for Draco's death. In her mind she knew if they were the ones responsible, they weren't going to live to tell about it. Though she wanted a lot of people dead, Draco wasn't one of them. She had a lot of respect for Draco and the respect she had for him he had earned every bit of it. One night she had tried to seduce him so she could brainwash him like the other men she had brainwashed, but Draco wasn't going for it. He had so much loyalty to Dunkin that he couldn't go behind his back and sleep with his baby mama. For some reason she liked that because most men took pussy over anything. Those same men who took pussy over anything were the same ones who Lisa never respected. Lisa used pussy whipped niggas to her advantage and made their dumb asses do whatever she wanted.

CHAPTER 6

Dunkin got off his flight in Indianapolis undetected. All he wanted to do was go home, get his guns, and call a meeting with Zynika, Terrance, and Nicole. He stayed low key his whole way home, instead of calling someone to pick him up he ordered an Uber. Dunkin's mind was all over the place. The only thing he knew he had to do was kill. As he rode in the back of the Uber looking over the lovely city of Indianapolis none of his thoughts were lovely at all.

When he arrived at his house nothing looked out of the ordinary. A couple neighbors waved at him as usual. Everything looked like it did before he went to Jamaica. Dunkin knew Milly probably didn't know anything about Draco dying because he never allowed her to be around anyone. Neither did Milly know anything about the stash house he had on the side. She was blind to pretty much everything he had going on except for spending money. He got to the door and unlocked it. As soon as he opened the door and stepped in the house, he looked and dropped all his luggage.

"Baby, what the fuck is going on," asked Dunkin as he ran to Milly?

She was still unconscious, so Dunkin didn't get a reply. He pulled out his iPhone to call the ambulance immediately and checked her pulse to see if she was breathing. Though she had been laying there for more than a day she was still breathing. Dunkin was now shitty all over again because he didn't know what was wrong with Milly.

While the ambulance were on the way he went upstairs to check out the rest of his house. When he opened his bedroom door his dog ran up to him still shaking in fear. He read the words, "Dunkin you're a dead man" written on his dog in permanent black marker. The words on his dog wasn't the end of the messages whoever it was that ambushed his house wanted him to see. The words, "Dunkin's final countdown" was written on all four walls of his bedroom. There was a calendar on the mirror written in permanent black marker as well. On the date of June twenty fifth it was written, "your last day living bitch." Dunkin was now even more shitty; it was June thirteenth at the time.

After seeing the messages Dunkin started to throw everything in the room. He had never had the problems he was having now. The only thing he could come up with was that it was somebody in Indianapolis who wanted his spot in the drug game. With no one in mind to blame he figured he would start with his crew. In his mind he believed someone in his crew was leaking information because he never let any outsiders know where he lived at. He ran back downstairs where Milly laid on the floor at because the ambulance had finally pulled up. He knew they would ask many questions, but he had no answers to give them, he was totally clueless.

No sooner than they got Milly on the ambulance Dunkin's phone started to ring. He answered the phone with an attitude asking, "what's up right now is not the time for me to talk NuNu?"

"This is about your kid's Dunkin. They were tied up last night and had guns drawn on them. They boarded Dexter's house up and left them tied up in the house to die, they even cut the wires to all the electricity in the house. Whoever the bastards was they left a message for you saying you would be dying soon. I don't know what to do Dunkin, you know we have never experienced this before. Tamara is terrified," said NuNu as she talked fast in fear.

"What! Some motherfuckers are about to die," yelled Dunkin into the phone!

"That's easy to say Dunkin, but who knows who it is," asked NuNu?

"Where are my babies at, NuNu," asked Dunkin as he put his head in his palm in disbelief?

“They all refused to go to the hospital, so they over here at my house now. I had my brother go over there and take them boards off all the windows and the doors. Then my uncle said he would go over there in a little while to connect the electricity,” said NuNu as she popped her gum in the phone.

“I’m on my way over there,” said Dunkin.

“How long will you be, I got company,” asked NuNu?

“Bitch this is about my kids, I could give a fuck less about your company. I’ll come in and kill his bitch ass the way I’m feeling right now please don’t go there with me,” replied Dunkin.

“Whatever, we are here. You know I would never let nothing come between you and your kids,” said NuNu as she started to think about how her and Dunkin used to make love. In her mind no man could ever replace him.

After hanging up the phone NuNu immediately went to her room and told Fat Boy he had to leave her house. Fat Boy was shitty at first, but after she told him what happened to her kids he understood and told her to call him if she needed any help. Fat Boy put on his clothes, shoes, and jewelry then left the house. Fat Boy wanted NuNu to be his woman so bad but knew with Dunkin in the way that would never happen. He would have married NuNu in the drop of a dime that's how much he loved her and though he knew she loved him; he knew she loved Dunkin more. Fat Boy had a plan to kill Dunkin so he could be with NuNu, but he knew he could never let her find out.

Dunkin's and Tyrea's personal trainer Eric was scrolling through Facebook on his laptop computer when he seen a message request from messenger pop up in his notifications. He clicked on the profile and knew who it was right off the top. It was Big Sam the prejudice white man from prison that he turned out to be friends with after what seemed like a lifetime of problems. Over the years of being released they still stayed in contact, but with the way Eric changed up Facebook pages no one could keep ahold of him. Eric read Big Sam's message and replied to it. Big Sam sent his number to Eric and told him to call him immediately.

"What's up my brother? Long time no hear. How have you been," said Eric as he talked to Big Sam.

"Nothing my brother. Just thought I would give you a call and of course you know your best brother needs a favor," said Big Sam as he laughed in the phone.

"I figured so, what you need bro I got you," asked Eric?

"You know I'll never even attempt to get you to trade on your people, but you know I've traded on mine for you. I have a problem with a guy by the name of Dunkin up your way. He has destroyed my daughter

Heather's life. Though I'm mad as fuck it doesn't have to lead to violence, I want to talk to him. Maybe he can talk to her and let her know that relationships don't work out all the time. And just because their relationship ended doesn't mean she has to give up on life and turn to doing drugs," pleaded Big Sam.

"Well, I happen to know him very well Sam. I train him. I will give him a call as soon as we get off the phone. He's a pretty good guy, but he does have a little thing for women. I will talk to him for you and see if I can schedule a meeting. I know exactly where you're coming from my brother. I couldn't even imagine my daughter going off the deep end, I'd be running around ready to kill something," said Eric.

"Glad you understand. At first, I was angry, but I can't be mad at a man because he wanted to get his dick wet and the lousy whore thought it was more. Thanks just give me a call. We will have to meet up for lunch this week too," said Sam.

"We definitely will, and I will call Dunkin now," said Eric as he hung up the phone.

Big Sam had no intention of just talking to Dunkin. He wanted to not just kill Dunkin, but he wanted to hang him by his toes while he was still alive. If Eric had to lose his life in the process for trying to protect Dunkin, then Big Sam didn't care. He felt no one had the right to do his daughter the way Dunkin had done her under any circumstance. Big Sam knew Eric wasn't a dummy, so he knew he had to choose his battle wisely.

After hanging up the phone Eric just sat there and thought about Dunkin and all the women, he had heard him talk about in his personal training sessions. Eric knew that Dunkin would fuck Big Sam up, but he also knew that Big Sam would give him a run for his money. Either way he knew he had to talk to Dunkin about the situation as soon as he could. Eric knew Dunkin had a lot going on and didn't want to burden him with anything else. He also knew he had to say something before things got out of hand and Big Sam caught him slipping.

After Lisa's meeting with Tyler and Doo Doo, she knew they had nothing to do with the hit at Dunkin's stash house, now she just wondered who it was that did it. This caught her by surprise because of all the years she had known Dunkin no one had the balls to run up in one of his houses. She was starting to think it was some dudes from out of town who did it, but then she thought not. Whoever it was she knew the streets of Indianapolis would probably never know. The fact that they didn't take any money or drugs was what made her wonder the most. She then felt it had to be another woman out to get him, but the question of who it was left her puzzled.

Lisa stripped down after deep thought and took a steamy hot shower. She had a television embedded into her shower wall, so she turned on a porn movie trying to clear her mind while she showered. Her beautiful features were hard to resist by any man, but the only man she wanted was Dunkin. She knew she would probably never have him back, but she was going to make him suffer for his childish ways. She figured after she had the baby, she would have more time with him and maybe things would change. From experience she knew Dunkin's actions were so unpredictable that she wouldn't know until the time was to come. With what she had just told Tyler and Doo Doo to do, she knew it would make Dunkin suffer. She put her all into making sure her request was going to get done right by letting Tyler and Doo Doo both run a train on her for the fee. She let Tyler and Doo Doo have their way with her because she felt pussy was a small price to pay for someone to take a life. Plus, she knew after they were done with all she wanted them to do she would kill them anyway.

Zynika, Terrance, and Nicole got to NuNu's house before Dunkin did. Dunkin had told them to meet him over there so they could all try to get to the bottom of what was going on. He checked on his mother, father and sister to make sure they were cool as well. He was headed to NuNu's before he got a call on the phone from Community North Hospital. They informed him that Milly would be okay and that she was pregnant at the time of going into her light coma. The man on the phone questioned Dunkin asking him why he wasn't there to support his woman as she was going through a horrible time in life. Dunkin told him to mind his fucking business before he came up to the hospital and fucked him up. The doctor apologized to him and told him that it would just be right for him to be there with Milly. He told Dunkin he felt bad because she had no one by her side. That's when Dunkin called his crew and NuNu and told them he would be arriving a little late.

The excitement in Dunkin's voice when he told NuNu he had another baby on the way and it was by Milly made NuNu get pissed off. She was pissed because she wondered how he could leave his first children for a baby on the way knowing what his children had just went through. Then when he explained to her that Milly was ambushed at their house, she understood why it was important for him to call the meeting off for a while. She knew with Zynika, Terrance, and Nicole at the house with her she was protected anyway. She was just startled by the news that someone had even went to Dunkin's house and she knew he never let anyone know where he lived at. She didn't know what Dunkin was up against, but she knew he was in for a battle. Then she thought again about the fact that whoever was doing all these things they never took money, drugs, or property. NuNu knew Dunkin was a soldier, but she also knew Dunkin's life was up for grabs.

Dunkin got to the hospital and went to the room with Milly. She was happy to see his face and for once in her relationship with Dunkin she felt he was by her side. He looked her in the eyes and just thought to himself that he loved her with all his life. He knew he had taken Milly through a lot of stuff and now that he knew she was pregnant he felt he needed to lighten up with all his bullshit. He was now ready to man up and be a family man. He looked at how beautiful Milly was and thought to himself that he had to be a fool for cheating on her with the women he had cheated on her with. Though he loved Abayomi he knew his heart was with Milly as he sat there and looked into her eyes. Then the way her face lit up when she seen him only made him feel more important to her life. In his heart he knew he would kill whoever was responsible for the things that occurred especially with his woman and his children.

As he stood next to her bed side his phone began to ring. He looked at it and seen it was Eric calling, so he didn't answer the phone. Then Eric called right back. Dunkin showed Milly that it wasn't a woman calling which he had never done before and then told her he had to step out to talk. She smiled at him and just by her facial expression he knew she was pleased. Dunkin now knew that he was in love because he had never asked any woman for permission to step out and talk on the phone.

"Hey, what's up big brother," asked Dunkin as he answered the phone?

"Nothing really, it's important that I talk to you in person like right now. Where are you at," asked Eric?

"I'm at the hospital with Milly bro a bunch of shit has been going on and I'm really just happy she is still alive right now. Along with my children, but I did lose one of my homeboy's. I don't know what to do big bro, but I'm at Community North you can come up here," replied Dunkin.

"Say no more, lil bro, I'm on my way," said Eric as he hung up the phone. Eric was really puzzled about what was going on because last he heard Dunkin was in Jamaica. He was surprised that Dunkin even answered the phone. Whatever was going on he felt he needed to tell Dunkin what Big Sam had just told him.

When Eric got to the hospital, he called Dunkin for him to come out and take a walk with him. Eric knew what was going on with Dunkin but knew Dunkin could be stubborn at times and not listen to his advice. With the sound of Dunkin's voice on the phone Eric felt Dunkin was at a breaking point, so he had to be there for him. He had been training Dunkin for years and Dunkin paid him very good for his training classes. It was Dunkin who paid cash for Eric's new fitness studio and wouldn't take no money back in return nor would he take a discount for any of his classes. Eric wasn't into taking nothing for free from anyone, but Dunkin kind of forced him to take his contribution. For that along with other reasons Eric could never turn on Dunkin and would do anything to keep him safe.

"Man, how are you? And how's the wife to be," asked Eric as he walked beside Dunkin?

"Not too good big bro somebody broke in my house and fucked Milly up. Then somebody went to my son's house while my other two kids were there and held them all at gunpoint. Then at my house with my crew some people ran in there with Ku Klux Klan gowns on and killed my homie Draco. The funny part is that no one took any money in none of the incidents. They all left a message that they were out to kill me though. They even wrote that I was a dead man with a black marker on my dog and all over my bedroom walls," said Dunkin as he looked at Eric like he had every answer he needed.

"I'm going to tell you something Dunkin and I want you to listen very carefully. I think it's one of these women whose heart you might have broken playing these games with you. I'm saying this for a reason, so you must hear me out. This situation is something that you know no man would ever attempt to commit with you. It's a scorned woman and it's no telling who she has riding with her on this mission," said Eric.

"So, you're telling me a bitch is responsible for all this," asked Dunkin?

"I got a call from a white dude I did time with back in the day earlier today. It was funny because he asked me about you. He didn't know that I knew you, but he knows I know a lot of people in the city and asked me to find you. His name is Big Sam and I think his daughter's name is Heather. He said he only wanted to talk to you because you broke his daughter's heart and now, she's strung out on drugs. He said he feels you can talk some sense into her even if you're not trying to be with her. I know this white boy too good and he's not just trying to talk. I know he's not a true threat, but you never know what's going on in the mind of a prejudice white boy," said Eric.

"Heather is the white bitch I brought to the gym with me that day that was a stripper, remember I told you her name was Passion? It's that cracker who has done all this shit, no wonder they had on Ku Klux Klan gowns when they ran in my house. I need his information I'm about to go kill him now. And I'm going to kill the bitch Passion too," replied Dunkin.

Eric stopped walking and talked to Dunkin about the fact that Big Sam would have never called him if he was the one behind the ambushes. Then Dunkin told Eric that he didn't know how he would have found out where his main house was at because he never let Passion know. Dunkin also told him that Passion never knew where his stash house was located at neither. After going over many scenarios Eric told Dunkin to attend to his woman and he would get back with him later. Eric had his mind made up that he was about to figure some things out.

Only thing Dunkin knew was that someone was going to pay for what had happened to his people. He was thankful for Eric because he was the one who made him see things from different angles. Dunkin had been thinking it was a nigga in the streets, but now he knew it could have been a bitch in the streets.

Dunkin spent more time with Milly. Milly had never seen the side of Dunkin she was now seeing. It was like he really loved her for once and she was loving every minute of it. Dunkin called his parents to come up to the hospital with Milly because he had some things he needed to do. He needed to be at NuNu's house immediately to check on his children and he also needed to console his crew. Though he was still thinking in the back of his mind that someone in his crew was working with the enemy. After his parents got to the hospital, he gave them a hug and told them he loved them before leaving. They didn't even know about what happened to his kids yet and he didn't want to bother them with it because he had to go. His sister Tyrea was also with his parents and for the first time in years they kissed and hugged each other and told each other they loved one another. After his family didn't act surprised about Milly being pregnant, he knew they must have talked already, which made him mad, but he let it go.

CHAPTER 7

Dunkin walked up to his BMW X5 SUV in the parking garage of Community North Hospital. His only plans was to go to NuNu's house to talk to his kids and then find out where Big Sam was living. He wanted to take his crew with him to go holler at Big Sam. No matter what Eric said Dunkin felt in his heart that Big Sam was the man behind the attacks. When Eric told him, he felt his beef was coming from a woman Dunkin felt Eric was right. However, Dunkin didn't feel it was a woman doing it herself, he felt it was someone who loved Passion doing the damage. Passion called Dunkin daily begging him to take her back. Dunkin was beginning to think that she was only calling him to set him up to be killed.

Dunkin turned on his SUV and was proceeding to take off, but his whole SUV dropped to the ground as soon as it moved. He slammed it back in park and jumped out the SUV. As soon as his feet hit the ground a white KIA Sportage SUV pulled up before he could come to his senses. He couldn't see what they were doing and then he started to get hit by paintballs in his face and all over his body. Dunkin opened his car door back up, but by the time he retrieved his gun the SUV was gone in the wind. One thing he did remember about the people in the SUV is that they had Ku Klux Klan masks on their faces.

By the time Dunkin was able to get himself together he was sitting in a hospital bed next to Milly. Of all the places they could have been together they were in the hospital together getting treated for some injuries that Dunkin was really the root problem of. Before you knew it, the whole hospital room was filled up. Even Lisa came to the hospital to see Dunkin. Though she couldn't do what she wanted to do with him she still went to show her baby father she had love for him. Milly disliked Lisa's presence being in the room. After about an hour of visiting the hospital security escorted everyone out the hospital room because they were being too loud. No one could believe someone had taken all the lug nuts off Dunkin's rims and shot him with paint balls instead of killing him. It didn't take a rocket scientist to figure out someone wanted him to suffer.

Dunkin had enough time to tell Zynika, Terrance, and Nicole the news that Eric had told him before they were put out his hospital room. None of them liked what they heard from Dunkin. They felt just like Dunkin felt and that was like the white boy had done everything. Terrance wanted to find Passion and he knew just where to find her at. They weren't taking nothing that happened in the past couple weeks lightly. It was a life for a life and an eye for an eye in their eyes. It was time for them to strike back and no one was off limits.

Lisa pulled back up to her house and wondered where all the attacks were coming from on Dunkin.

Then when she found out Milly was in the hospital; she knew something was up, but she couldn't figure out who would have been behind the attacks. She was happy that Dunkin was suffering, but she wanted to be the person who caused his pain and suffering. She knew that NuNu couldn't have been behind the attacks because she loved Dunkin too much, plus her kids were attacked too. Only thing on Lisa's mind was getting in on the fun. She was losing sleep every night and knew the only way she could sleep well was if she brought pain to Dunkin.

Lisa sat back for the night. She figured she would watch some movies and catch up on the phone with some of her cousins from Ohio. She was watching "Waiting to Exhale" until she got bored with it, she then changed the channel from the movie to a porn video. Lisa was a freak, but she really didn't like men like that. She just gave them pussy for them to do what she wanted them to do, but when she really wanted to be pleased, she pleased herself. Overall, she did good for herself independently, but that didn't stop men from buying her many expensive gifts. She stayed in a four thousand square foot house and had every feature in it to make you think she lived in a mansion in Malibu somewhere. She also had four expensive cars to go with her expensive house. Her candy red Lexus LS500 had twenty-four-inch Forgiato rims on it and a sound system. Then she had an Escalade, a limited-edition CTS sports coupe Cadillac, and a brand-new Challenger. She was doing her thing to the fullest that's why she didn't know why she couldn't let Dunkin go so easy. Then she thought to herself that it was because he was the only man, she had really given her heart to. She never had true feelings for a man until Dunkin came along.

Lisa laid there in her bed watching the porn video for long enough she thought. It was time for her to please herself. She grabbed her biggest dildo off her nightstand. She was about the only woman you would catch with her dildo's out in the open and didn't care who seen them. She didn't care who knew she was a freak. She played with her clit for a few minutes with her fingers before inserting the dildo into her moist warm pussy. She tried to pull it back out, but it wouldn't come out. That's when her closet door busted open and she seen a face, she was very familiar with.

"Bitch, you like to go fucking every man so how about you die with a dick in you. You and your baby about to die bitch," said the woman standing over Lisa.

"Fuck you, you don't come in my house thinking you can get over on me. You on my homecourt bitch," said Lisa as she reached under her pillow for her gun that wasn't there. When Lisa figured out who was standing over her, she was in shock. At first, she thought it was just a dream, then she knew it wasn't, but it was too late for her to talk.

"I been in and out your house for the last eight days watching your every move. Hope you didn't think I'd be stupid enough to super glue a dildo in you on your bed and leave a gun under your pillow," said the woman as she held up Lisa's gun that she looked for under her pillow.

That's when Lisa started to scream, but what she didn't know is that she was sedated. The sedation she was injected with made it where she could feel and see everything, but she couldn't talk. Even though her mouth would move there was no words she could say. Her pussy was shut off completely with the dildo super glued to her inside pussy walls. Then the lady took out Lisa's second to biggest dildo and soaked it in super glue before plunging it into Lisa's mouth. Now her mouth had a dildo super glued in it too. Then for the finale the lady soaked another dildo in super glue and shoved it up Lisa's ass after turning her on her side.

"Bitch see whose man you can fuck now. I let your pretty ass slide long enough and I didn't come for no rap this time bitch, shouldn't have fucked with mine. Dunkin is mine, I can't believe you really thought I liked you, just stupid," said the lady as she laughed.

That's when the woman pulled out a black marker and wrote the words, "I tried to let the baby live you dirty motherfucker, you know I love you Dunkin" on Lisa's stomach. After that she took Lisa's own gun and shot Lisa in the stomach. Lisa laid there lifeless on the bed, butt naked after the fatal shot from her own gun. The woman then grabbed Lisa's iPhone and Facetimed Dunkin. When Dunkin saw Lisa's body on the Facetime video he went into shock.

Milly looked over at Dunkin with a confused look on her face before she jumped to her feet. She grabbed the phone and when she seen the horrific scene she screamed. The voice in the background on the phone said, "one by one." Then the phone hung up.

Milly called the police and sent them to Lisa's house. Though Milly didn't care too much for Lisa she didn't want to see any woman get done the way she had just seen Lisa done on the phone. She figured it had to be a cold-hearted person to do that to a woman and shoot an unborn baby. In all of Milly's years of living she had never seen or heard a story quite like the one she was witnessing. Her seeing the dildo's in Lisa's mouth, pussy, and ass made her stomach get upset. She didn't know the most crucial part about the dildo's and that was that they were super glued into Lisa.

Dunkin got his composure under control and told Milly he was leaving the hospital. She tried to tell him she thought he needed to stay, but Dunkin wasn't trying to hear a word. He was fed up, so he only told Milly to be quiet. His mission was to kill from that moment forward. He knew now that it had to be Passion's father behind everything. Dunkin was thankful for Eric putting him up on game, but he didn't want to hear anything else from Eric other than where Big Sam lived.

"Baby, you stay here until the doctor's tell you it's time for you to go. I can't take a chance of you leaving here with my baby in your stomach and something happening to you. Right now, I think this is the safest place for you to be," said Dunkin as he looked Milly in the eyes with a look of concern.

"I want to go with you. I feel too afraid to let you leave by yourself Dunkin. I can't lose you, please stay here with me at least until you're officially released from the hospital," begged Milly.

"Milly you see what's going on. I must get out of here and see what I can figure out. This is no time for games, somebody is out to kill me, but I promise you I will kill them first," replied Dunkin as he left out the hospital room before waiting to hear a reply.

Dunkin had already told Terrance to bring him another car to the hospital. He told Terrance to bring his

Audi Q7 SUV to the hospital because no one had ever seen him in his Audi before. Terrance did exactly what he told him to do and left the keys under the mat. The Audi didn't need a key to start but needed the keypad in the car to start and it had keyless entry. Dunkin didn't know where he was going after he got in his car, but he knew he needed to smoke a blunt real fast before he went crazy. He was afraid to go home because it was dark outside, but he would never let anyone know he was afraid. Dunkin had pounds of loud at home, but he knew he couldn't go so he decided he was going to stop in his neighborhood to grab a sack.

Right when Dunkin got to the stoplight on 38th and Emerson Avenue the police surrounded his SUV. He was right around the corner from his hood. He didn't know what the fuck was going on, but the way things had been going nothing surprised him about his luck. A police officer started talking to him from the intercom connected to his police car. He ordered him to get out his car and to walk backwards to his squad car. Dunkin knew this only usually happened when you were driving a stolen car. Once Dunkin got to the back of his SUV, he could see what happened and why the police used precaution. Someone had switched the license plates on his vehicle. He only put D.A.R.E. plates on all his cars but the plates on his car now were an old version of regular Indiana plates. He seen the plates were at least two to three years outdated, but the question was how they got on his car.

"Man, what the fuck do you crackers want with me? I'm not out here doing shit," said Dunkin as his tall body stood over the cops.

"All so you must like the nigger side of your family more you piece of shit ass half breed. We don't accept you anyway with your tainted blood. I should lock you up right now and then go rape your bitch," said the smart mouth cop as the other cops started to laugh.

"Fuck you bitches what do you dick suckers want," asked Dunkin with anger in his voice?

"Well, you can start off by telling us how you know India Reeves. Your plates are registered to a woman who disappeared without a trace almost three years ago," said the cop.

"What in the fuck, she was one of my exes and I don't know how her old plates would have gotten on my car because they never found her vehicle after she went missing neither," answered Dunkin.

"Well, we will have to take you down to headquarters for questioning. After all you may be a murderer you nigger. I guess this cracker just put some salt on your next move," said the cop as he laughed.

"I just bought this car a few months ago and I've only drove it maybe four times. There is no way this could be going on. Someone is playing tricks on me. I have shit to do, don't take me to that funky ass county," said Dunkin.

"Our captain will be pulling up in a few minutes so you can talk to him all about that, but if it was up to me, I'd be charging you with murder right now for the disappearance of India Reeves. I'm starting to remember about this disappearance now and you did it," said the smart mouth cop.

After the captain of the police department pulled on the scene and talked to Dunkin, he knew someone had to be trying to pull a set up on Dunkin. The car came back registered to Dunkin, but no one knew how the plates would have gotten on Dunkin's car. Then on top of that, India's car was never found. Now they were thinking that India was somewhere around, and they needed to find her. She disappeared from her family almost three years before this incident. No one knew if she was dead or alive. All they knew now was that it was a lot of explaining for someone to do.

India was a woman Dunkin had messed around with for years before her disappearance. After he told her he didn't want to mess around with her anymore her behavior started to change, and she eventually disappeared. Everyone thought she had committed suicide somewhere because of Dunkin and for that reason her family didn't like Dunkin. Her family didn't know that Dunkin really loved India though. The main reason why India's family was upset with Dunkin and Lisa is because it wasn't long after India disappeared that Lisa started messing around with Dunkin. They were mad because Lisa and India were best friends before India's disappearance, they had been best friends since high school. People were running around Indianapolis saying that Dunkin and Lisa killed India so they could be together. Lisa was also the only one who knew about India being pregnant at the time of her disappearance.

The police impounded Dunkin's SUV and let him leave the scene but told him the detectives would be contacting him very soon. The whole situation made

Dunkin feel uneasy. He hadn't seen India in years and always wondered if she was dead or alive. He couldn't believe the license plates from her old car that was never found ended up on his car. For some strange reason he felt she was still alive, and she was the person behind the murder of Lisa. He just couldn't figure out why she would disappear so long and then come back to kill. It now made sense to Dunkin what Eric had said to him a few days earlier. Now he really felt like it was a woman whose heart he had broken, after him, but it still didn't make any sense.

The news about what happened to Lisa was starting to hit the streets and it made a lot of people mad. No one knew the other side of Lisa that some others knew, so many thought she was a good girl. They just didn't know that she was the one trying to have Dunkin's whole family killed. Nor knew that she was the one on the low moving bricks of cocaine. No one would have ever imagined that she was letting so many men fuck her while she was pregnant with Dunkin's baby neither. There was a lot of shit many people didn't know about Lisa. Yet and still no one wanted to see her go out the way she went out.

"Man, what the fuck are we going to do without her," asked Doo Doo as he cried like a baby about Lisa getting killed?

"I don't know man. I just want to die bro. I don't know what we will do without her," answered Tyler as he cried like a baby too.

None of Lisa's other goons was attached to her like Tyler and Doo Doo were. They both genuinely loved Lisa to death. If she was looking over them after her death, she would have cried too by how sad they were about her being gone. There was no question that Lisa had them both pussy whipped. They were just some suckers in love with a woman who suckered them.

“Bro we have to carry out every wish she had before she died,” said Tyler.

“I know! I want Dunkin dead because I know he had this done to her,” replied Doo Doo.

“We going to kill that pretty boy ass fag ass bitch ass nigga bro and for the first time I feel like killing his sister too just like Lisa wanted,” said Tyler.

“I never knew I was in love with Lisa until now. I miss her already,” said Doo Doo.

“We gone do this shit for Lisa bro and there is no turning back. Dunkin bitch ass than made the wrong move with this one,” said Tyler as he wiped tears off his face.

“I never want to touch another woman again bro,” said Doo Doo as he started to cry again.

“Say no more bro you know what we got to do,” said Tyler as he got up to leave.

Doo Doo let Tyler leave. He planned for them to be meeting back up after a few hours in order to start the execution of Dunkin. Doo Doo went to his CD player and turned on a song called “I miss you” by a singer named Joe. He sat there letting the music play, but the words from “I miss you” didn’t make his mood any better. You would have thought Doo Doo was married to Lisa by the way he was taking her death. Not long after he sat down to listen to the music, he was on his feet walking to his bedroom. He had sixty Perc tens on his dresser and slammed most of them down his throat before picking up his bottle of D’usse to chase them down.

Before he went to sleep for his last time while breathing, he said, “Lisa baby, I’m coming to be with you.” Those were the last words he said before he stopped breathing.

CHAPTER 8

"NuNu I need you to come get me now, I don't know what type of creepy shit is going on, but we need to talk. I'm on Butler and the police than took my car," said Dunkin as he waited on a reply from NuNu.

"I'm on my way to get you now," said NuNu as she grabbed the keys to her old school box Chevy sitting on thirty-inch rims. Her choice of car on this day was flashy.

NuNu had a lot going on in her mind. She knew at the end of the day that Dunkin trusted her more than any woman he had ever been involved with. After all they had spent many years together and she had his first three children. The secrets she held of Dunkin would send him to prison for the rest of his life if she were to tell them. No matter what man she loved she knew she would be there for Dunkin in any way she could so him calling her to come get him only made her happy. NuNu knew that Dunkin would be upset with the news about Lisa being killed. It made her sad too because she never wanted to see any woman be done the way Lisa was done. She felt whoever it was should have just shot Lisa and got it over with, so she wouldn't have had to suffer.

After picking up Dunkin NuNu explained to him how everything happened with his children. As she explained Dunkin just continued to get madder and madder. He couldn't believe someone had gotten so close that they could have murdered his children. Of all his years in the game he had never touched a child and never had plans of doing such a thing. Through all the talking Dunkin couldn't help but to look at NuNu and think about how proud he was of her for everything she had accomplished since they had broken up. Sitting in her box Chevy made him think of when she couldn't stand him riding on rims. He laughed in his own mind about the fact that she used to tell him they were too flashy and now she put rims on every car she owned.

"We will get to the kids in a minute. Pull this motherfucker over. I want you to really feel like a boss bitch by letting me suck on them toes and eat that pussy right here in this front seat," said Dunkin as he stared at NuNu.

"Well, if you say it like that then I'm pulling this thang on over then baby daddy," said NuNu as she smiled.

Her heart was still with Dunkin. Though they didn't have sex or anything often she still loved every time they did. She knew Dunkin loved to suck on her toes. NuNu used to tease Dunkin sometimes by wearing open toed heels knowing he would want to suck her toes on site. He worshipped her feet more than any woman's feet on earth. She remembered when he would ask her to sleep upside down so he could have her feet in his face the whole night. NuNu laughed every time she thought about him telling her to sleep upside down.

They pulled into a parking space at the gas station. They pulled in so no one could see them through the windshield. Dunkin immediately unzipped his pants and NuNu immediately tried to grab his dick to start giving him head. Dunkin stopped her right in her tracks and turned her body around while at the same time putting her toes in his mouth. With his other hand he fingered her pussy as she closed her eyes. The tight mini skirt NuNu wore gave Dunkin easy access to the goods he cherished on NuNu.

"Oh, my god I love you," said NuNu as she enjoyed her toes being sucked.

After sucking her toes Dunkin told NuNu to turn around. No sooner than she turned around he had his whole tongue in her asshole. NuNu almost knocked Dunkin out as she bounced her big ass butt cheeks back into his face. That was one thing Dunkin loved about Nunu, the way she fucked back. Dunkin went from licking her asshole to licking her pussy for about forty-five minutes before he wiped his mouth off and sat back in the passenger seat of her car. She then tried to give him head again, but he told her no and to jack his dick off with her feet instead. NuNu moved her feet up and down on his dick for about twenty strokes before Dunkin busted a nut all over her feet. She then sucked his dick to get all the rest of the nut out of his nut sack. After that NuNu pulled some weed out to roll up a blunt.

"Damn I'm glad you brought a sack with you, shit that's what I was on my way to get before the police started fuckin with me," said Dunkin.

"You know I stay with a sack baby and this shit is hitting good. What is going on though Dunkin? Why did the police take your car," asked NuNu as she stared at Dunkin with a concerned look on her face?

That's when Dunkin started to explain to her that India's license plates was on his car and he didn't have a clue how they would have gotten there. He also told her that he believed India's family could have had something to do with Lisa's death. He told her that he knew in his heart India was dead so he knew she couldn't have been behind anything in any way. NuNu told him that she felt India was dead as well, but it wouldn't surprise her if she was still alive. He told her if it wasn't for her and his kids, he would tell Milly to pack her shit and they would move out of town.

They sat there talking and smoking until NuNu seen Fat Boy's car pull up with a woman in the car with him. He didn't see her because she was ducked off on the side. The thing was that she couldn't confront Fat Boy in front of Dunkin. She knew Dunkin would get pissed off and probably kill them both. He knew NuNu messed around with Fat Boy, but not to the extreme that she would be mad about him being with another woman. That's when Dunkin looked in the direction of Fat Boy.

"That's your boyfriend over there ain't it," asked Dunkin as he started to giggle?

"He's a friend punk shut up," answered NuNu as they both started to laugh.

That's when Dunkin seen Vikeya get out of Fat Boy's car. Vikeya was a woman Dunkin used to date who was mixed with Japanese and Black. Out of all the women Dunkin had been with no woman had ever left him heartbroken like Vikeya did. She had an attitude just like a nigga and didn't play any games. Dunkin was a man who wasn't ready for a woman like Vikeya, she looked good and didn't mind letting a man know that she didn't sweat no nigga. For some reason seeing Vikeya get out of Fat Boy's Monte Carlo sitting on them twenty-six-inch rims made Dunkin get pissed off. He had just talked to her a few days before and she swore up and down she wasn't fucking nobody.

"I guess this fat ass nigga just fuck all my ex bitches," said Dunkin as the smile on his face was wiped away with a frown. He didn't care who Fat Boy fucked, but when it came to Vikeya it was a different story.

"Dunkin it's hard for somebody not to fuck a bitch you than been with. You know you than fucked every bitch in Indianapolis. You than had ugly bitches, bad bitches, and all the rest of the bitches in between. Quit tripping about that bitch Dunkin, she ain't shit," said NuNu as she too was shitty but didn't want to let it out.

As NuNu and Dunkin were talking Fat Boy looked around to be aware of his surroundings like any drug dealer would and that's when he seen NuNu's car ducked off to the side. He tried to play it off like he didn't see it, but then wondered what the hell she was doing at the gas station. It was late and she was driving her toy on top of that, Fat Boy wanted to know what was up. Vikeya got out the car to go into the gas station and as she walked, she turned every nigga head on the gas station parking lot. Her nickname was "ass everywhere" because she literally had "ass everywhere." Fat Boy went to sit back in his car and as soon as he sat down, he pulled his iPhone out to call NuNu.

"Hello," said NuNu.

"Damn baby you sound sexy. Where you at," asked Fat Boy?

"Shit up here at Citgo with Dunkin, smoking on this blunt. What you got up," replied NuNu as she passed the blunt back to Dunkin? The whole time Dunkin was laughing to himself. He knew she messed around with Fat Boy, but he didn't like nobody calling his baby mama "baby."

"All okay, I'm up here too and thought I saw your car. Holler at me if you need me. I see you're with the love of your life and don't want to disturb you. I don't want Pretty Ricky getting mad at me," said Fat Boy as he started to giggle.

As soon as Dunkin heard the slick remark, he jumped out of NuNu's car and headed over to Fat Boy's car. Dunkin had been waiting for his chance to beat the fuck out of Fat Boy. He found out about Fat Boy dealing with NuNu from Draco. Ever since the day he had found out he was looking for any reason to have an altercation with him. He didn't want to be beefing with no nigga about a woman but that was the reason for his beef.

"Nigga I'll show your bitch ass a Pretty Ricky with your fat ass, funky motherfucker," said Dunkin as he walked up to Fat Boy's car and opened his car door up.

Dunkin had never really had a problem with Fat Boy before, but he always kept an eye out for him. Fat Boy was the type to want to be in control of everything and from experience Dunkin knew that would cause a person to plot. Dunkin knew that Fat Boy had his own army of people, but if it wasn't for Dunkin none of them would have been eating in the streets. Fat Boy's army knew this and for that reason alone Dunkin kept the upper hand in the situation. All Fat Boy's people wanted to be down with Dunkin and even Fat Boy knew this about his crew.

"Man, bro what's the problem," asked Fat Boy as he got out of his car?

"I'm none of your bro, I just heard that bitch ass shit you said on the phone to my bitch though so give me a one on one fade bitch ass nigga nobody going to jump in this shit," said Dunkin. And by this time there was a crowd around them both. Though none of the people around were too concerned with the wellbeing of Fat Boy. It seemed that everyone had their camera phones out trying to take pictures of Dunkin.

"I'm not going to get in a fight I can't win bro. You got me and I apologize for saying that bullshit on the phone," said Fat Boy.

After Fat Boy said that Vikeya was walking back up to the car and NuNu was getting out of her car to see what was going on. People were yelling that Fat Boy was a punk and calling him all kind of names, but Dunkin just stared him in the eyes. The look he gave him wasn't a look of madness though, instead it was a look of amazement. Fat Boy had killed Dunkin with kindness, and this gave Fat Boy the upper hand.

"All you nosey bitch ass niggas and bitches get the fuck away from here and find you some business to attend to before I have your families start planning your funerals," said Dunkin. Once Dunkin said that to the crowd, they all dispersed. No one in Indianapolis had the power Dunkin had, and he made sure he let others know it when he had to.

"What the fuck is going on out here? Dunkin you need to get off your bullshit you're always starting something because you got people scared of you. That's why I could never fuck with you like that again. You're too fucking arrogant," said Vikeya.

"Bitch, what you mean fuck with me like that? Bitch last I remember you was sucking my dick and drinking my nut like Kool Aid, so don't get beside yourself slutty bitch," said Dunkin.

"Yeah okay whatever," said Vikeya. She wasn't expecting Dunkin to put her on blast like he did, so she just shut her mouth. Then on top of that she seen NuNu standing there and knew she didn't like her, so she just got quiet.

"Yeah bitch that's your best bet to get quiet," said NuNu.

"Fat Boy come take a walk with me just down the sidewalk and back," said Dunkin as he looked at Fat Boy. Dunkin said that before Vikeya responded to NuNu because he knew if she said the wrong thing NuNu would have beat her ass.

Fat Boy hesitated because he didn't know if Dunkin was up to something, but he did go.

"Bro, what you just did was probably the most honorable shit I've ever seen in life. For a man to apologize it really means a lot and I've been struggling with apologizing for years. As a matter of fact, I've never apologized to a soul in my life," said Dunkin.

"You know my father told me growing up that it takes a man to apologize, but it takes an even bigger man to accept an apology, so I give you mad love for accepting my apology," responded Fat Boy.

Dunkin and Fat Boy stood across the street from the gas station talking in the parking lot of a tire shop for about an hour or so. By the time the conversation was over with, Fat Boy had him a new plug and a new low price on cocaine, heroin, and weed. He also had the promise that he would become a part of Dunkin's inner circle if he could just stay low key for a while. They talked about NuNu and Dunkin told Fat Boy that he didn't care who he fucked. He also told Fat Boy to not let who he was fucking come between his money and his respect in the streets. Just trying to give him game.

NuNu sat across the street staring and wondering what they were talking about. She just knew they were over there talking about her like she was a dog. She also knew that they both thought just alike, so she knew they would end up talking about business as well. NuNu only fell for Fat Boy because he reminded her so much of Dunkin when it came to money. It wasn't nothing for Fat Boy to give her a hundred thousand to hold for him and not come back to get it for weeks sometimes. From her experience in the game she knew if a person could just leave money like that sitting around, they had to be playing with some real money.

"Bitch find you a ride dumb bitch," said Fat Boy as he looked Vikeya in the face. For some reason Fat Boy felt like he needed to let her go. He wanted to do it in Dunkin's face to show him he wouldn't let a woman come between him and his money.

"So, you going to play me like that you fat funky no neck ass motherfucker. That's why your shoes leaning now you fat bitch. Fuck you this is where I'm from I will find a ride and you make sure you never call my number again. I should have my brother take your shit you punk," said Vikeya as she turned around to walk away.

"So, you going to have somebody take something from me bitch," asked Fat Boy as he grabbed his handgun out of his car?

"You must think I'm scared of a fat no neck boy with a gun," replied Vikeya as she laughed at Fat Boy. NuNu couldn't help but to laugh herself.

"I really don't know what you are, but dead people usually don't have no sense of humor," said Fat Boy as he shot Vikeya in her head.

After the shooting everyone at the gas station left the scene, many of them burned rubber getting away from the scene. The only thing left on the lot of the gas station when the police arrived was the lifeless body of Vikeya. Dunkin applauded Fat Boy for what he had done to Vikeya because she threatened him with robbery. Dunkin knew he would have done the same exact thing as Fat Boy, but he would have probably shot her more than once. In the game once a threat was made no matter by who, it had to be handled. In their eyes Vikeya was capable of anything for even mentioning robbing a man she was just fucking.

NuNu and Dunkin were on their way back to NuNu's house when her phone rang. She seen it was Fat Boy and ignored it because she wanted to holler at him when Dunkin wasn't around. She knew she needed to talk to Dunkin about the way she felt about Fat Boy. NuNu knew Dunkin would understand, but she also knew it could cause a problem. From experience NuNu knew that any woman could fuck business up when it came to men doing business. Especially if both men had ties to the same woman. She wanted to get things clear with Dunkin before he even started to do business with Fat Boy.

After getting to NuNu's house Dunkin gave his children a hug and began to ask them about what happened the night they were ambushed. They told him everything, but still the weird part to him was that the people didn't look for money or drugs. Dunkin thought about the same thing when Draco was killed at his stash house, no one took money or drugs there neither. In his mind he knew for a fact it was him they were looking for, but they wanted him to suffer before they killed him. So, he knew he had to find Big Sam first because he knew that it was him behind everything. The main reason he knew it was Big Sam is because of the KKK gowns.

Dunkin had a long talk with his kids that night and a talk with NuNu as well. It was like Dunkin was getting all his karma in a way he never expected. He slept in NuNu's guest room on this night and thought about life for hours. Him watching Law & Order SVU only made him go back to before he started in the game and how simple life was back then. Now he had killed his best friend, lost a good friend plus a baby mama, and his kids along with his other baby mama were assaulted. He felt life couldn't get any worst, but knew once he got things settled, he was leaving Indianapolis for good. Now his biggest decision to make was if he was going to be with Milly or Abayomi.

NuNu laid in bed that night with a bittersweet type feeling. She was proud of Dunkin for finally seeing things someone else's way other than his own. And the talk he had with her about Fat Boy really blew her mind. Dunkin said that he honored and respected Fat Boy because he apologized for his wrong even after he was called out of his name. NuNu knew from experience that Dunkin usually looked at people who apologized like they were weak, but now he was honoring Fat Boy for apologizing. Any other night Dunkin would have slept in the bed with NuNu, but this night he told her he didn't want to. Only because he felt she had feelings for Fat Boy and should give him a fair chance. Which was a total surprise because the whole time NuNu and Dunkin were together he couldn't help but to fuck her to sleep every time he saw her in black lingerie. NuNu tried to turn him on by putting on black lingerie and having half her ass coming out the bottom of the panties, but on this night, Dunkin was being a gentleman.

Meanwhile Fat Boy was out riding around sad because he thought the woman, he loved was in the house getting dicked down by Dunkin. Fat Boy wasn't no punk, but he knew not to cross the line with Dunkin unless he was catching him slipping. He felt if Dunkin was going to plug him that he was going to take him up on his offer and just let things be the way they had to be with NuNu. Deep down he knew that she loved Dunkin. He wasn't going to trip about something that was put together before he was in the picture. As bad as he wanted to though, he couldn't let the love of his life fuck another man so easily.

CHAPTER 9

"You bitch ass punk ass cracker," said Dunkin as he continuously punched Big Sam in the face with his fist wrapped in brass knuckles.

It had been a long two weeks for Dunkin to get ahold of Big Sam and Passion. As soon as they were in his possession, he didn't waste any time starting his torture tactics. Dunkin felt that Big Sam had committed the ultimate sin when he went messing with his children. Though he was shitty about everything else the fact that he fucked with his children put him over the top. Terrance had told Dunkin that he was going to find Passion and he did just that. Not only did he find her and Big Sam, but he also found Big Sam's wife, his brother along with his wife, and Big Sam's other daughter too. Dunkin took them to his house in a town called Westfield, Indiana where no one would hear their screams. Dunkin knew his five acres of land in

Westfield was the perfect place because no one came on the property.

"Fuck you nigger. I had no need to touch your fucking kids, your wife or your family," said Big Sam as he spit blood out his mouth.

"Yeah, well it's too late for that punk ass cracker I got the juice and always had the juice," said Dunkin as he bent Passion and Big Sam's other daughter over at the same time.

Dunkin was taking his time raping them back and forth. Big Sam almost died just looking at the scene and then the ultimate happened. Dunkin grabbed Big Sam's wife and his brother's wife to dick them down as well. After putting his two daughters to the side he made Big Sam's wife and brothers wife give him head as he laid on a pallet made on the floor. Every woman in the room seemed to enjoy Dunkin though. The women just pleaded with Dunkin begging him not to kill them. Telling him they knew for sure Big Sam wasn't behind the attacks.

"I swear to gawd I didn't do anything to your family please let my people go. Do what you want to me, but please let them go," said Big Sam as he cried for the first time in his adulthood. The scene of his family being raped before his eyes was the worst feeling he ever felt in life.

"It's too late for all that white boy, I'm enjoying this pussy and head. You tried to fuck over me but now I'm fucking over you literally. Got yo ass sounding like a preacher or some shit talking about let my people go," said Dunkin as he pushed the other women to the side and plunged his dick back into Big Sam's other daughter's throat. The whole time Dunkin had a smile on his face.

The rest of the women begged Dunkin to join in and get some of the action as Big Sam's other daughter gave him head. They were being raped but they were enjoying the dick. They fucked for hours. Moaning and having orgasms right in front of Big Sam and his brother's faces. The rest of the women told Passion that they could see why she fell for Dunkin because his black dick was good. Terrance was upstairs watching television the whole time like nothing was going on in the basement. Dunkin had also called Eric to come to the house because that was the only way Big Sam's life could be spared. Eric would have to give Dunkin a good enough reason to let Big Sam live.

"Please keep us as sex slaves. I will help on bills and everything. I have plenty money in the bank that I can spend however I want. I just want to be with you the rest of my life. I'll give you all I have. I have inheritance money too," said Big Sam's sister in law as she tried to grab Dunkin's dick to suck some more.

"Bitch shut up," said Dunkin as he slapped her to the ground.

"Yes, daddy I obey your order, but I want you. And by the way I love it ruff like you're giving it to me daddy," said Big Sam's sister in law again in a lustful way.

That's when Dunkin walked with his naked body over to his gun and once, he picked it up, he shot Big Sam's brother right in his face. Big Sam cried like a baby as his brother laid there with blood pouring out his head. His little brother looked up to him so much and he protected his brother, but at this time he was tied up and beaten half to death. There was no protection he could give his brother and he couldn't live with the thought.

"Just fucking kill me you nigger, please. And all of you sluts can rot in hell you nigger loving bitches. I will see you all again in the afterlife and I promise to kill you whether we are in heaven or hell," said Big Sam as he tried his best to get loose from the restraints Dunkin had placed on him.

"I'll tell you what I'm a do to you boy. I'm a make one of your people kill you. As a matter of fact, the bitch who started this shit will do it. Your daughter will kill you bitch. Now you'll know to never cross a nigga named Dunkin when you get to hell you bitch ass cracker. And fuck you again cracker," said Dunkin as he looked in the direction of Passion.

Passion thought Dunkin was playing around, but he wasn't at all. He wanted Big Sam to suffer for what he did to his family. He felt in his heart that Passion was the one who killed Lisa, so he wanted her to suffer from killing her father for as long as she lived. He knew the only way he could leave the women alive was if he caged them in his house because they could go to the police if they got loose. Dunkin didn't want to kill the women because the sex was too good. He loved the thought of having sex slaves.

Dunkin paced around the room. His mind was all over the place. The women had their eyes glued on him the entire time just admiring his body. He was happy to be able to have control of the whole situation because he was a control freak. Not even Dunkin himself knew he could be so evil, but he couldn't let his feelings stop him from being evil. Big Sam had to pay and that was the only thing on Dunkin's mind.

"Bitch get up," said Dunkin as he finally quit pacing the room and was ready to make a move.

"Please don't make me do it, please," pleaded Passion as he handed her a gun and held another gun to her head. The other women thought about attacking him, but he was too big for them and he had a gun, so they chose to look at the ground instead.

"Put the fucking gun to his head dumb bitch before I kill all you dumb ass crackers you white trash ass bitches," said Dunkin.

"I'd rather just die then Dunkin I can't do it. I promise you my dad has done nothing to your family. He may have wanted to hurt just you, not your family, but he never did anything. He had no way of finding no one in your family. Me and you dated for a while and I don't even know how to find your family. Please don't make me do this Dunkin," begged Passion.

"Bitch you come over here and get ready for this dick," said Dunkin as he looked at Big Sam's wife which was Passion's mother.

"Please don't hurt me. I will do anything you want me to do," begged Passion's mother as she looked Dunkin in the eyes.

"Get down and get ready to take this dick doggy style. Sammy boy I want your last vision before you die to be me fucking your wife while your own daughter is killing you. After this I will let you hoes go. If you ever choose to call any police, I won't be found by them and I will find every one of you bitches again and finish you like I should do now," said Dunkin.

Big Sam's brother's wife sat there and all she could do was cry. Though the sex was good from

Dunkin she could see that he was an evil person. She knew she had never felt fear like that in her life and as she looked at her husband dead on the floor, she had no feelings. Her feelings went numb as she stared into space. The whole time she was sitting there Dunkin was contemplating his next move. He really wanted to let them go including Big Sam but knew he would be risking going to prison. He felt he could let the women go free, but if Big Sam went free, he knew he was risking prison. On top of going to prison he knew with Big Sam loose, he risked getting caught slipping by a white supremacist gang. He couldn't risk his freedom and life like that, so he knew Big Sam had to die.

"Bitch shoot him in the head before I shoot your mother in her head and then shoot you in yours after that. None of this shit would be happening if you had of just went on by your business when I was done with your pussy, but your bitch ass wanted to be a pest. Now it has led to all of this," said Dunkin as he penetrated

Passion's mother in the ass and held the gun to Passion's head at the same time. She let out plenty moans and with every moan a tear came out of her and Big Sam's eyes.

"Why me? Please Heather just fucking kill me, please just kill me. I can't take this anymore. Lord I'm sorry for everything I've done I know I didn't do anything bad enough to deserve this but just let me rest in peace," pleaded Big Sam.

After pleading Big Sam had a vision of the day, he had to kill a black man while in prison. The words the man told him before he took his last breath were coming to haunt him like the man said. Rodney was a forty-eight-year-old black man from Alabama who really minded his business at the high security prison they were at serving time. Though the man had committed a crime he was a model inmate during his whole incarceration. He was due to be released from prison in four days, but Big Sam killed him before his release date. Rodney's family awaited him in Alabama and some of his family had already traveled to Indiana for his release to take him back to Alabama.

The Aryan Brotherhood had put a hit out on Rodney because they thought he stole some pouches of Tobacco off the recreation yard. Rodney worked the yard and was the only one on the football field the day the Tobacco was planted. All of Rodney's black people pretty much turned their backs on him because the unity within the black people wasn't united at all at this prison. Big Sam used to be cool with Rodney and Big Sam stood up for him when he said he didn't take the package. Though Big Sam was the president of the Aryan's he still had to put in work if it was his turn and he was the one who was voted in to do the dirt on this occasion. After Big Sam stood up for Rodney his brothers called him a nigger lover. They told Big Sam if he didn't put in work on Rodney, they would put work in on him and he knew that meant they would take him out the game.

Rodney went into the laundry room in his dormitory on this day and that's where Big Sam caught him slipping at. Big Sam first hit him with a lock in a sock then pulled out his shank and began to stab Rodney. Once Rodney hit the floor Big Sam got on top of him and stabbed him repeatedly. Big Sam stopped stabbing him when he seen that Rodney was losing consciousness. That's when Rodney said his last words to Big Sam. Rodney spoke his last words to Big Sam sounding country as hell,

"Sam you know I didn't steal them cigarettes. You and your family will suffer for taking me away from my family. God don't like ugly Sam."

"Kill that motherfucker right now. I mean right fucking now bitch," said Dunkin as he continued to fuck Passion's mother in the ass harder and harder.

Those were the words that brought Big Sam out of his daydream as he thought about Rodney. Big Sam did feel bad for what he had done to Rodney. Then to make it so bad they found out the package that was supposedly stolen was never even dropped off in the first place. Big Sam found out who Rodney's family was and used to send them anonymous checks in the mail all the time. There was nothing he could do to give them what they really wanted, which was Rodney and he felt bad for that. Big Sam did make it around to kill all the men who made him kill Rodney, he felt that was the only right thing to do.

"Please don't make me, please I'll suck your toes," said Passion as she began to lower the pistol to her side.

As she said those words Dunkin began to bust a nut inside of her mother's ass. Right while he was busting the nut in her he shot her in the back of the head. Big Sam started going crazy then. He almost broke all the restraints he had placed on him. His burst of strength was cut short when another gun shot was heard. The gun shot sound came from Dunkin shooting Big Sam's brother's wife in the head as she sat on the ground Indian style. Passion then shot her father in the head thinking it would make her life be spared. Big Sam finally hit the ground after the dead weight of his heavy body broke the wooden chair Dunkin had restrained him to. Before Big Sam died, he thought he had a chance of living because he had broken his leg restraints and stood on his feet. His hope was cut short after Passion shot him square in the head. The whole basement was now bloody with Dunkin and Passion being the only ones in the basement still living.

"Now bitch get over here and suck my dick. You said you wanted me so now you got me," said Dunkin as he took his gun back from Passion and smacked her across the face.

"I can't Dunkin, I just can't, you just killed my family right in my face and made me kill my own father. Please just let me leave I promise I will never tell on you. I have a child I want to live to see every day. I was in love with you that's the only reason I was so messed up after you left me. I never meant to cause harm on your life or no one else's life," said Passion as she fell to the ground and continued to cry.

"I guess you're with your family now then bitch," said Dunkin as he shot her brains out.

When Terrance and Eric seen what Dunkin had done, they just stared at him like he was a ghost. Dunkin had finally calmed down and then started to laugh at them when he seen the expressions on their faces. They knew they had a mess to clean up, but the good thing was that no one had a clue the bodies would have been at Dunkin's house. When Eric pulled up to the house, he had no idea what he was walking into. As soon as he stepped in the house, he could smell death even standing upstairs. Once he entered the basement, he thought it may have been animals in there because of the gruesome scene.

"Well, I guess my family will be at peace now that these crackers are gone," said Dunkin as he walked upstairs to take a shower.

"Yeah, I guess so," said Terrance and Eric at the same time while shaking their heads.

Dunkin had got to the top of the staircase and then turned around to go back downstairs. As soon as he seen his gun, he picked it up and shot Eric in the head.

"Man, what the fuck? You're losing your fucking mind man he was cool as fuck," said Terrance as he made sure he had his hand close to his pistol.

CHAPTER 10

Dunkin, Terrance, Nicole and Zynika chose to go out to have a few drinks. Of all people to meet them there Zynika and Terrance didn't think it would be Fat Boy. A few weeks had passed, and the crew was seeming to get things back together for the most part with their normal drug operations. Milly was still in the hospital, but she was looking to be released in the next few days. Dunkin was planning a trip back to Jamaica to see Abayomi. He knew the visit would be his last visit to Abayomi because he made his mind up that he was going to be faithful to Milly and raise his child the right way.

Lisa had a safe deposit box when she died. One of her nieces had the key to it and went to get Lisa's belongings out after she died. The safe deposit box contained jewelry, cash, car titles, a note to Dunkin, and a song on a CD for Dunkin. When Dunkin received the note, he got upset and sad at the same time. One reason he was upset was because of his unborn child being killed. The song she wrote for him had an R and B rhythm to it. Dunkin shed tears after reading the note and listening to the song. Dunkin was starting to feel like a piece of shit. The song he heard from Lisa made him want to go away and hide. He knew she loved him, and he had never heard love expressed to him genuinely through a song. He knew that Lisa could rap a little, but the song made him feel like she could have been on a major label. Dunkin knew he didn't have it in his heart to break another woman's heart from then on.

Dunkin went to sleep very well at night knowing that Big Sam was dead. He felt a sense of relief because he didn't have to worry about Big Sam bothering his family anymore. Most nights he was sleeping in the hospital room with Milly, but other than that he was home. The doctor was still holding Milly because her blood pressure hadn't gone down in weeks. Dunkin and his crew had bought another stash house that only they knew about, but NuNu and Fat Boy were also told the location. After the night Dunkin had talked to NuNu her and Fat Boy decided to give their relationship a real try. For once in NuNu's life since her separation from Dunkin she was happy. What made her even more happy is that Dunkin accepted Fat Boy.

Over the few weeks that passed Dunkin's youngest son Dexter graduated from IUPUI receiving his master's degree in business management. Though Dunkin went all out for his graduation by buying him a house Dunkin's father did something very special for his grandson. He gave Dexter his asphalt company which generated over a five hundred thousand dollar profit a year. Dunkin also sent Dexter and his other two children on vacation to Aruba so they could see how life was in another country. Plus, Dunkin felt they all deserved something nice after what Big Sam had put them through.

At the Roof Top which was a bar in downtown Indianapolis that usually attracted a big crowd on Thursday nights, Dunkin and the crew did it big. Dunkin bought the whole bar and let everyone who was there drink for free. They were on a roof so high that they could see all over the city of Indianapolis from it. Dunkin and his crew stood there looking over the city smoking a blunt like they were the kings and queens of Indianapolis. Then to make the night even more interesting Dunkin had helicopters deliver brand new Corvettes to Zynika, Terrance and Nicole right there on the roof. He just wanted to compensate them for the pain they went through while he was in Jamaica. His love was truly going to Nicole because he knew how close her, and her brother Draco was before his death. Part of the reason why he went so hard on Big Sam was because of Draco.

After the cars were delivered Dunkin went to the bar to get another shot of Don Julio. Anyone from

Indianapolis knew who Dunkin was for a fact. If a person was from out of town when they would see Dunkin, they knew off top he was a high-profile drug dealer. Dunkin was rocking a pair of white Amiri jeans with a white button up Amiri shirt to match. He had on a pair of customized white Jordan's that even Jordan himself had seen on Twitter and gave Dunkin his props for designing them. Jordan was so intrigued that he asked Dunkin for ideas for new shoes he was releasing. Dunkin had on a platinum necklace, with a bracelet and watch to match. To top it off he had a real two carat diamond embedded into the middle of his forehead for the night.

"I don't care what you do for a living or if you're married or not, I want to fuck you and I want to fuck you now," said Alexis a woman who just walked up to Dunkin at the bar out of nowhere. She was a short dark-skinned woman with a pretty face and fat ass.

Many people said that Alexis looked like a darker version of Rhianna.

"Well, damn are you going to ask me my name first," asked Dunkin as he giggled?

Though he was trying to do the right thing with Milly he couldn't resist a pretty woman. How Alexis came to him was nothing new to him, he was used to women dropping their panties for him at the drop of a dime. As he stood there staring at Alexis, he was already imagining her naked.

"Shit, I'm from out of town I don't got a second to waste. I'm feeling this liquor, this weed, now I need to feel you with your fine ass. Then you got pretty ass teeth too, damn let's go," said Alexis as she grabbed Dunkin by the hand after feeling on his manhood.

"Just take my number, I can't go right this minute. I'm here with my crew having a good time and it would be rude for me to leave right now. You're more than welcome to come join us at our table though," offered Dunkin as he tried to control himself because he wanted to fuck her right that minute.

After Dunkin introduced Alexis at the table one of her friends walked up and introduced herself. She was a cold piece too. Terrance was about to try to get on her, but Nicole beat him to the punch. Nicole got next to her and ordered her a drink real quick then started a conversation. Nicole figured she deserved to have a good time with a beautiful woman after all she had been through. Terrance started texting Nicole's phone while at the table joking with her calling her a wool licker. She laughed and told him they could pass the hoe around.

After leaving the Roof Top Dunkin took Alexis to the JW Marriot located in downtown Indianapolis as well. Dunkin fucked her so good that she told him she wasn't going back home in St. Louis until the following week. He was impressed by her because she was a woman, but still a boss. When she told him, she was going to stay in Indy she immediately got on the phone and started giving orders. Alexis went as far as to tell somebody to go pick her dog up so she could make sure her dog was eating good while she was gone.

Dunkin took Alexis everywhere he went for a couple days he also took her shopping since she was staying extra days. She told him she didn't need him to take her shopping, but he insisted on paying for her clothes. Dunkin had showed her all of Indianapolis and put Milly's calls on do not disturb. He slowly felt himself going back to his old ways, but he didn't care because he was with a pretty woman. He was in love with the way Alexis's pussy tasted. To him her pussy tasted like butter scotch. When he asked her about it, she told him it was her favorite candy, so she ate it a lot. She also told him that her pussy was all his if he wanted it.

Whenever Alexis asked Dunkin anything about his personal life, he never answered her questions. As far as she knew he was just a successful man in real estate. Alexis wasn't new to the game though she knew he was in the streets in some type of way. She seen all the respect he received from everyone in the club and witnessed him have brand new Corvettes delivered to his crew. She knew he was a big boy to have the cars delivered by helicopter. She didn't really give a fuck about his money though; she just wanted some dick.

After another day of Alexis getting to know Indianapolis Dunkin took her back to their downtown hotel room. As soon as they got in the door they started kissing. Dunkin had secretly bought holding straps for them to use during sex. Alexis didn't know but she was in for the ride of her life.

"I don't know what type of kinky shit you're into when it comes to sex, but I got to take you to another level. I want you to strap me down, so I'll be your slave for a little while," said Dunkin.

"Well, I see that you a freak freak I like that shit nigga," said Alexis as she laughed at Dunkin.

"Shit I'm trying to make sure I'm always on your mind when you go back to St. Louis. A woman of your status deserve to have it your way all the time. I want to stick my tongue so far in your pussy that my tongue will be able to massage your heart to heal any brokenness you may have felt in the past," said Dunkin as he moved closer and kissed Alexis.

"I'm just in this for the sex my guy. All that broken heart shit is for the bitches that need a nigga, but bitches like me just want a nigga around when we want one," said Alexis.

"Well bend over and let me lick all in that ass hole then boss bitch. I need to go grocery shopping anyway," said Dunkin.

"Let me lick yours first," said Alexis.

"Hell naw what type of shit you on? I'm a man bitch," said Dunkin.

"Don't think I was trying to be disrespectful, but I feel that an ass hole is no place to be for a tongue. I've had it done before, but I don't respect a man who will degrade himself like that," said Alexis.

"I'm a freak and I like eating thick bitches' asses. You don't have to respect me at all, I just want to eat that ass baby," said Dunkin as they both started to laugh.

"With that being said, come on and eat away then nigga," said Alexis as she bent over and her ass cheeks spread apart.

Dunkin ate her ass for about fifteen minutes before he told her to strap him down. After she strapped him down to each of the four bed posts, he told her to sit on his face. He demanded her to not get up until he told her to get up. Alexis was thinking that she missed out by not visiting Indianapolis a long time ago. If she had of known the niggas was freaks like Dunkin was demonstrating, she would have been in Indy a long time before she came. She had never had a nigga in St. Louis please her like this Nap town nigga. She got her pussy ate, ass ate, and rode his dick all night. When she would try to give him head, he would tell her to stop and just enjoy being pleased. The night ended with Dunkin sleep while still strapped up and her laid out sleep next to him with her ass smeared to the side of his face.

The next morning Dunkin woke up to a big surprise. Alexis was nowhere to be found but she left him a message on the mirror. Dunkin immediately checked his pockets and all his money was still there. Then he looked and seen that his jewelry was still there. Afterwards he finally read the message she left on the mirror for him to read. It said,

"No this isn't a message telling you I gave you some horrible disease or nothing, I just want to thank you for a very good time. The sex was truly amazing. I gave you the wrong number because I never want to see you again and that's not a bad thing. I'm just on some me shit in life currently. I left you a thousand dollars in the drawer under this message for your lovely tongue because that motherfucker worked wonders on a bitch. Have a good one and if it's meant to meet again you know we will. I unstrapped you because I'm not on no bullshit."

Dunkin thought to himself that he had never been treated that way, he felt like a used slut. He knew he was lucky that she didn't steal all his shit and leave him strapped up. He did try calling the number she left him, and it was a fake number just like she said. Dunkin was so surprised that he laid back down and went to sleep. For some reason he knew he would never forget her sexy ass. She was gone and he didn't even have a picture with her which made him sad.

As Dunkin sat there his phone began to ring. His heart skipped a beat because he hoped it was Alexis calling him to tell him she was playing and just went out for a little while. His hope was cut short when he seen the phone number and knew it was a hospital call from Milly. When he answered she told him she was due to be released the next morning. Milly told him that she didn't want to go to their normal house she instead wanted to stay in one of their rental properties. Dunkin had no problem with her request being that he felt some type of way being there himself. He figured he would just get the house together and put it up for sale. Dunkin knew that the life he wanted to live with Milly would cause him to put a lot of things from the past in the past.

CHAPTER 11

The sun was just starting to go down and Dunkin was feeling anxious about Milly being released from the hospital the next morning. He went back to their house to take a shower and pick up a few personal belongings to carry along. The people he hired to fix the house from the incident with Milly had done a great job. Dunkin had them put new cameras up in the inside and outside of the house, there was even a camera on the mailbox that sat out on the street. He really didn't want to leave his house and knew the only way he could get Milly to stay was by making her feel secure. He had gotten rid of the dogs and was on the hunt for new and more vicious dogs. He felt Milly should have never got attacked with a dog in the house.

Dunkin turned on the surround sound in the master bedroom so he could hop in the shower. Every inch of the room vibrated due to the high-performance stereo system. Every room in their house had its own set of speakers for surround sound and had the option of playing different audio. He turned on NBA Youngboy from the shower controller and began to take his shower. After standing under the hot steamy water for about five minutes he squirted a few squirts of Irish Spring body wash onto his sponge. He then began to wash himself. "Survivor" was his favorite song by NBA Youngboy and it banged through the speakers. He was grooving so hard to the music that his shower cap almost came off his head and exposed his braids. Dunkin never let his braids get wet so he would have been shitty if that happened.

Dunkin was rinsing his face wash off his face when he thought he heard a sound. As soon as he opened his eyes, he knew he had seen a body figure run past the doorway of his master bedroom. Then he thought that he was tripping. Unlike most master bedroom bathrooms, Dunkin's sat in the middle of the bedroom surrounded by all glass and gold trimming.

The glass was only high enough to keep the water from splashing onto the carpet of the bedroom. He used to love sitting back in their Whirlpool Jet Spa Bathtub watching Milly take a shower under the skylight in the middle of their bedroom. Most of the time he wouldn't be able to resist himself and would start jacking off while Milly was showering. It was starting to set in on Dunkin that he was missing Milly and missing her badly. He still knew he had to end things with Abayomi, but he was going to go to Jamaica and do it like a man. Though he could have just disappeared on Abayomi because she didn't know where he stayed. Abayomi had no way to contact him if he didn't contact her first.

The steam was gushing out the shower. The glass around the shower only went neck high on Dunkin. Suddenly the music changed that was playing from his speakers. He didn't know how the fuck it was happening, but it was. All he could now hear coming from the speakers was, “you gone cry, you gone pay me in tears. You gone cry; you owe me for all these years. You gone cry, you gone suffer.” He knew it was something weird going on right that minute. For sure he knew he didn’t have not one K Michelle song programmed in his phone. Just as he turned the water off a full bottle of Modelo beer was thrown from nowhere and it busted one of his pieces of glass surrounding the shower.

He jumped out the shower while watching for glass and went to retrieve one of his rifles. Dunkin had guns planted all around his house. As soon as he grabbed his AR-15 assault rifle he started to shoot in every direction. He could hear noise from downstairs, so he started to go in that direction. Dunkin wasn’t scared by a long shot. Once he hit the bottom stair, he could see his front door was wide opened. He grabbed a robe and headed outside because he knew the police were on the way. One of his neighbors walked up to him and told him he seen someone running from his house in a KKK gown. When Dunkin heard that he was lost for words.

After talking to the police and neighbors Dunkin called Zynika on the phone. He told her what had just went on and she was totally clueless about the situation as well. They both thought the problem was gone once he killed Big Sam, but the problem was far from gone. The rest of the crew was about to be shitty. Especially Terrance because he was the only one who knew that Dunkin had killed Eric for no reason. Dunkin had a flashback of the night he made Big Sam and his family suffer. He seen Eric's face as well and thought to himself that he was wrong for killing Eric. Dunkin's conscious was telling him that he murdered Eric for nothing. The only reason he murdered Eric is because he thought he was the one who told Big Sam all the information he needed about the locations that were attacked. Now he was seeing it had to have been someone different from Big Sam who was attacking him in the first place.

Now the only thought on Dunkin's mind was getting to the hospital with Milly. He started up his Porsche 911 and headed to the hospital. Lil Wayne's song "six foot seven foot" bumped out of Dunkin's speakers as he sped to the hospital anxious to see Milly. Dunkin knew he couldn't leave Milly alone in the hospital after someone was just in their house again. He figured he would stay at the hospital with her until the morning when she was released and then head out of town with her to lay low. Shit was getting out of hand and the only way to get on top of things was to watch from a distance. Zynika sent the word to the rest of the crew of what happened to Dunkin. When Terrance and Nicole found out they all split up to go and make sure everyone's family was safe. Dunkin had enough sense in his head to call Fat Boy and ask him to keep an eye on his kids and NuNu. Fat Boy told him he would and asked him if there was anything else, he needed.

Upon arriving to the hospital Dunkin could tell something wasn't right when he first got on the floor of Milly's room. Nurses and doctors were running everywhere and there was a whole squad of police standing outside of Milly's room. As soon as Dunkin seen the police he ran to the room. In his heart he knew something was wrong and felt bad immediately. Dunkin knew he was wrong for not being at the hospital with Milly in the first place.

"Sir hold it right here," said the officer as he grabbed Dunkin to stop him from going in Milly's room.

"What the fuck you mean nigga? My girl and my baby in there," said Dunkin as he still tried to get past the officer.

"You need to sit the fuck down," said another cop as he assisted the other cop with getting Dunkin under control.

"Please give him a break officer. He has been at this hospital many times I know who he is. He has been through enough," said Sara the pretty nurse.

"Well, I can't let no one go into there. This is a crime scene not a family reunion," said the cop.

"What the fuck do you mean crime scene," asked Dunkin as he made another attempt to get past the cops? Dunkin was now angry.

Two doctors walked up to the door and asked Dunkin to come with them and then they motioned for the cops to come with them as well. Dunkin was bracing himself for the worst. He could tell by the way the nurse and doctors looked that something bad had happened. He knew the cops didn't give a shit about nobody so their expressions didn't tell him anything.

Right when he thought about that he seen a chaplain and his heart dropped right at that moment.

"Would you like water, tea, or coffee," asked the doctor as he looked at Dunkin with a tear coming from his eye?

"I don't want nothing, but to know what the fuck is going on. You dick sucking motherfuckers need to tell me what the fuck is going on," said Dunkin as he demanded answers.

"I'm pretty sure you refer to her as Milly. I'm here to tell you that she is in a coma that she may not recover from. And the sad news is that your child didn't make it," said the doctor.

"Nooooo. Please tell me what happened. This can't be true," said Dunkin as he dropped to his knees and put his hands up like he was praying.

"A lady dressed as a nurse came into the hospital without no one noticing she didn't work here. Somehow, she was able to get a deadly dosage of fentanyl into your fiancée's IV. We checked, but the baby lost its heartbeat and Milly is liable to lose her heartbeat at any minute. We are so sorry to tell you this news. No one wanted to be the one to tell you, but I did because you should know what's going on. We do have a witness with a sketch artist right now trying to get a description of the suspect," said the doctor.

Dunkin passed out after the news of what had just happened to Milly and his unborn child. Dunkin passed out because of the news, but he also passed out because of guilt he felt. He remembered Milly telling him she didn't feel safe at the hospital alone. Of all the bad things in the world he had done, he never felt regret. He was now regretting his life totally. All he knew from that moment on was that someone was going to pay for what happened to Milly and his unborn child. Dunkin was now turning into a maniac.

The doctors then put Dunkin in a room of his own and asked the police to keep heavy security on him. While Dunkin was passed out Milly was in the next hospital room about to take her last breath. Her heartbeat was going in and out until there was a constant beeping sound on the heart monitor. Milly died while Dunkin was passed out, so he didn't know. Once he was awake and well the doctor's figured it would be a good time to let him know. Under his current conditions they knew some news like that would probably put him in a coma as well.

One of NuNu's friends who worked at the hospital seen Dunkin's name on the bed board and immediately called NuNu. NuNu's friend name was Cynthia and she had been with Dunkin a few times before herself. Dunkin begged NuNu to have a threesome with Cynthia and himself, after days of begging NuNu fell for it. After the threesome Dunkin used to hook up with Cynthia on his own. Cynthia had a husband at home, so she really didn't sweat Dunkin at all. However sometimes she would crave the dick and would then start blowing Dunkin's phone up on the late night.

When NuNu alerted Dunkin's crew they were all in a hurry to get to the hospital the only one she couldn't get in contact with was Zynika. Dunkin's parents and his sister were hysterical when they heard the news. His sister Tyrea told her parents she couldn't go to the hospital and see her brother in bad condition. She also told her parents that she couldn't see Milly deceased. Tyrea's mind was all over the place and she didn't know what to do. In her heart she knew her brother had brought the things going on upon himself, but she still didn't like the fact that other people were getting hurt as well. At this point Tyrea felt she had enough and was going to try to figure out who was behind all the killings, kidnappings and break ins. Meanwhile Dunkin's parents were speeding in their S550 Benz to get to the hospital to be with their son.

Zynika was with her son that no one knew about when NuNu was trying to call her, so she couldn't answer her phone even if she wanted to answer. She seen the call, but she hadn't seen her son in weeks and wanted to spend time with him. Zynika had no idea what was going on with Dunkin, but even if she did know she wasn't about to leave her son. Dunkin and Zynika had been best friends for years. Zynika was now starting to feel like she was letting Dunkin control her life too much. She was also secretly mad at Dunkin because he had fucked one of her bitches. She knew Dunkin had to of known she had feelings for the bitch, so she was shitty he still decided to fuck her anyway. Zynika held a resentment against Dunkin ever since he fucked her bitch Diana. Zynika paid Diana back by having her killed and no one knew she was the one who sent the hit out on Diana, but one person. Since Draco was dead no one was left on the earth who could ever let the secret out about the killing. The only reason

Draco knew about the hit is because Zynika paid him to fulfill the hit. Draco would have killed for her without being paid, but Zynika insisted on paying him.

Abayomi was back in Jamaica wondering what was going on with Dunkin. It wasn't like him to not answer her calls, so she was beginning to get worried. The only problem Abayomi now had was that she had no way of getting in contact with Dunkin. Dunkin never let her know anything about his family or his whereabouts. He never let her become friends with him on Facebook neither, which she found strange, but never questioned him. She waited patiently by her phone for his call with tears in her eyes praying he was safe. Her uncle had a voodoo shop at the Pavillion Mall there in Kingston, Jamaica. She wanted to give him a call just to see if he could possibly put a safety spell on Dunkin. She also wanted to see if he could find out Dunkin's whereabouts. Abayomi had her bags packed and ready to go to the Norman Manley International

Airport to head to the United States. She knew she wouldn't sleep until she knew he was okay, so she was determined to get to the United States to be next to Dunkin.

Back at Community North Hospital, Dunkin was starting to gain his consciousness back. He looked around at all the people in his hospital room. By the look on their faces he knew he was better off passing back out because there was bad news to come. Dunkin knew the look of bad news on his parents faces very well.

"Where is Milly at? Is she okay," asked Dunkin as he looked into his mothers' eyes?

"Dunkin, please just worry about yourself right now. The doctor's said you are on the verge of having a stroke," said his mother as she looked into her son's eyes.

"Ma, that's my fiancée I want to know what's going on. Pops would feel the same way about you.

Last I remember we were both in the same hospital room," said Dunkin.

"Dunkin, she took her last breath at 6:06 p.m. today. She is dead Dunkin, but I……" said Dunkin's mother before she was cut off in mid-sentence.

"No one will see me again until I kill whoever is responsible for this shit," said Dunkin as he got up and looked at everyone in the room.

The look Dunkin had in his eyes defined a man with murder on his mind. NuNu, Terrance, and Nicole looked at him and didn't say a word. They knew it wasn't a good time to talk to him and didn't want to upset him, so they kept their mouths shut. Since he was mad, they figured they would let him blow his steam off then talk to him afterwards. Everyone in the room felt bad for Dunkin. They knew his feelings were hurt because none of them had ever seen him sad.

Dunkin wasted no time ripping out his IV's and fleeing from the hospital. He didn't look for a ride or a car to drive when he exited the hospital. Dunkin just ran away from the hospital with no intentions of returning. He went to the apartments next to the hospital to sit by the lake and think about everything that had just happened. Dunkin was familiar with the apartments because he had a bachelor pad in them years before. Lake Castleton Apartments was low key, and he could see the hospital police from every direction if they tried to come for him. He wasn't normally a cigarette smoker, but he was looking for a cigarette on this day. As he sat there on the rock glaring over the water tears started to form in his eyes. After thinking for no more than five minutes he was crying like a baby. Dunkin had never questioned the reason why anything happened in his life, but on this day he did.

Cassandra was walking her dog through the apartments while smoking a cigarette when she heard Dunkin sobbing. She was going through some things herself that she couldn't cope with at all, so she felt his pain. Cassandra had just lost her mother and lost her son to CPS the same day, so the struggle was real for her too. She was just a little white girl who loved to party. She didn't have a dangerous bone in her body. Dunkin didn't even notice her walking up and didn't know she was there until he smelled the cigarette smoke.

"Move from the fuck around me," said Dunkin as he looked at Cassandra.

"Well you don't have to be a shit head. I just heard you over here crying and wanted to check on you. You know a man jumped in the water and killed himself last week, so I like to check on people when I see them going through stress and standing by the water," said Cassandra as she pulled her dress back down from the wind lifting it up.

"My bad, my day just isn't going good at all. I just lost my baby mama and my unborn child in her stomach over there at Community North," said Dunkin as he humbled himself and felt bad for cussing the lady out.

"I understand. I just lost my mother and CPS took my son because my ex-boyfriend called in and lied on me. So, it looks like we are both in the same situation. So sorry to hear your news though," said Cassandra as she patted Dunkin on the back.

"I just don't understand why it has to be me. I know I've done some things in life, but Milly was so innocent, and my child wasn't even here yet. They didn't deserve to die," said Dunkin as he leaned on Cassandra and started to cry again.

They then sat there at the lake talking about each other's problems. Dunkin had smoked three of Cassandra's cigarette's in under twenty minutes of them sitting at the lake. Really Dunkin had nowhere to go and nowhere to be, so sitting at the lake talking to a stranger was interesting to him. He didn't have no money to his name and didn't feel like he was broke.

Dunkin had money in his pockets for so long that he wanted to see how it felt to be broke and roam around the city with no car. Him and Cassandra had a lot in common and Dunkin respected her because she showed interest in him without knowing he had money. In Dunkin's heart he knew Cassandra had to be a good woman.

As the day turned to night Cassandra offered Dunkin to come to her place so he could get some sleep. Dunkin got up quick and told her he would take her up on her offer. Before he walked off, he threw his phone in the lake. Dunkin wanted to stay away from everyone at that time. He wasn't mad at anyone, but he felt he needed to be to himself. Cassandra still didn't know who he really was, and he didn't want her to know. He wanted someone to just know him for being an ordinary human being for once. Dunkin did make a mental note that he was going to look out for Cassandra real nice for showing him love though.

CHAPTER 12

Dunkin was awakened by Cassandra's music. "You make me feel like I'm living a teenage dream the way you turn me on," said Katy Perry as her music played out of Cassandra's stereo.

Dunkin had been at her house for two days straight. Her house was clean, and she had plenty food though they hadn't eaten anything the whole two days. Cassandra walked around her apartment freely in only her panties and bra. Though she was skinny she wasn't just skin and bones. She had a nice shape, but her and Dunkin weren't looking at each other on a sexual level. He walked around with only his boxers on, but never had an erection. Their minds were on other things far from sex.

"Damn, you up already," said Dunkin as he raised up from laying down on the couch. The only clothes Dunkin had was the hospital outfit he had on when he fled from the hospital.

"Well yeah I'm up. Are you ready to get started? We need to go to the bank so I can get some money," replied Cassandra.

Cassandra had access to all her deceased mother's money. Her mother had over fifty thousand dollars cash in her checking account when she died. Dunkin and Cassandra were spending up every penny of the money with the dope man. Cassandra got Dunkin to try some crack cocaine and after his first blast he never put the pipe down. Dunkin was sitting in her apartment looking like any other crackhead. He didn't look like the normal Dunkin at all. Not only were they smoking, but right after they hit the pipe, they would snort a line of raw cocaine. Dunkin had lost at least twenty pounds within the few days he had been with Cassandra. Dunkin never wanted to leave Cassandra's presence. They were having a lot of fun together. They couldn't believe they related on many levels when it came to life even though they had totally different backgrounds. They weren't the type of crackheads to just sit in the apartment smoking neither, they went out to smoke dope too. They went to the Canal and other public places as well just to hit the pipe. Dunkin never had to spend a dollar. Cassandra liked having a smoking partner and thought Dunkin was cool, so she didn't mind being the sole provider of their habit.

"Shit you know I'm ready. This shit got me feeling the best I've felt in years. It's like my problems don't even exist anymore. Mad at myself for not trying this shit before," said Dunkin as he put on the clothes Cassandra had bought him from Wal Mart. His hair was nappy, and he was musty, but he didn't give a fuck at the time.

Cassandra's 2002 Ford Taurus wasn't in the best condition, but it got them to the bank and wherever else they needed to go. Over the few days she had been with Dunkin she didn't answer her phone or the door to her apartment for no one. The people knocking at the door knew someone was in the apartment because they could hear people talking. Cassandra didn't care she felt she paid her own rent and didn't have to answer her door if she didn't want to. Dunkin stayed low key whenever she went to buy more drugs and knew every house, she pulled up on to buy the drugs. The five percent tinted windows on her car kept people from seeing Dunkin in the car. Dunkin thought Cassandra was the sexiest woman on earth when she hit the pipe. Her pink toenail polish matched the pink pipe she smoked her crack out of and that was the sexiest shit ever to Dunkin. He was turning into a full fledge crackhead. His people were out looking for him, but he was nowhere to be found.

When Cassandra went into Chase bank this time the teller informed her that a hold had been placed on her mother's account. They told her that the fifteen thousand dollars she had withdrawn from the account within three days was not normal activity for the account. The bank put a hold on the account to investigate the transactions, but Cassandra thought a family member had it done. Cassandra almost got arrested when they told her about the hold. She cussed out the teller and swung on the security guard when he tried to get her to leave the bank. Dunkin was sitting in the car waiting on her with the next hit of the pipe on his mind. He was going to tell her to stop at Wal Mart so he could get new boxers because he wanted red boxers to match his red crack pipe.

"What's up are you cool you look mad as fuck," asked Dunkin as he looked at Cassandra when she made her way back to the car?

"These fuckers won't let me get any money out the bank. They said I've withdrawn too much money out the account over the last couple days. I just want to die right now," said Cassandra.

“Don’t worry, I have a secret account that no one knows about. Just take me to PNC bank,” said Dunkin with a smile on his face.

“You fucking rock dude,” said Cassandra.

“I try my best,” said Dunkin as he smiled thinking about his next hit of the pipe.

Though Dunkin and Cassandra had been together a few days she still had no clue he was rich and the biggest drug dealer in Indianapolis. He felt when it was the right time, he would tell her who he was and where he came from. He felt like he had just found a lifelong friend when he found Cassandra. Dunkin knew he would have to face reality one day, but he wasn’t worried about that at the time. He knew Abayomi was probably worried about him, but he wasn’t worried about that neither. He had a “fuck the world” attitude to the fullest. He said fuck his kids, his parents, and everybody else.

"Yes, I need five thousand and my ending balance," said Dunkin as he talked to the bank teller. He had Cassandra take him to a bank far out so no one would notice him.

"Okay sir, and how would you like your money to be," asked the bank teller?

If Dunkin wasn't going through the things, he was going through he would have hollered at the teller for sure. She was a pretty little chocolate skinned woman with a nice shape. Dunkin always fell for the women who were professional, and she was as professional as a banker could come.

"Thanks, and I would like all hundred-dollar bills," replied Dunkin.

"Okay sir, here is your money and your ending balance. Is there anything else I can help you with? I see you made a big purchase on a house, congratulations," said the teller.

When the teller said something about the purchase of a house Dunkin looked at her very puzzled. After she said that he looked at his balance and seen that he only had five thousand dollars left in his account. He went into panic mode and wanted answers. He told the teller he wanted to know who went in his account because it wasn't him. Dunkin had never told a soul about this bank account. Now he knew that whoever was plotting the attacks on him had to be someone close because they had to have known his personal information to get access to his account. He just didn't have a clue of who it could have been.

Dunkin eventually just walked out of the bank. When Cassandra asked him, what took him so long he told her the line was long. Only thing on his mind at the time was getting some more crack and some more powder cocaine. The drugs made his mind go to a whole other level and that's the level he wanted to stay on. He gave Cassandra three thousand dollars and told her to put two of those thousands on crack and the other thousand on powder cocaine. His mind was set on taking a blast of the pipe and snorting a line. Cassandra had spent a lot of her own money on drugs, but she hadn't spent a whole three thousand at one time. She was ready to party, and she felt even better about Dunkin now because she could see he wasn't a user like all her other smoking buddies were.

"Can you suck my dick while I hit the pipe," asked Dunkin as he looked at Cassandra? They had just got back to the apartment and he was ready to get his smoke on and his freak on.

"Yes, I love to suck dick. I been wondering when you would ask to fuck me," said Cassandra as she reached down to unbuckle his pants. When she felt his dick, she closed her eyes and let out a moan because it was the biggest dick she ever touched, now her mind was on pleasing it.

"Well get to sucking then," demanded Dunkin as he put the pipe to his lips.

Dunkin sat back in the chair like he was a king sitting on his throne. He smoked his crack and got his dicked sucked and she sucked his dick better than he ever had it sucked before. Now he felt like he was going to ask her to marry him. The feeling he was feeling was that good. After he busted a nut in her mouth, and she swallowed every drop he told her to grab her pipe and sit in the chair. He told her he wanted to eat her pussy while she hit the pipe. Cassandra didn't refuse it neither she took her clothes and panties off and sat on the chair. Only thing the two were missing was a camera because they had a straight porn scene going on.

After their oral sex exchange, they continued to smoke and snort dope while listening to music. The powder was gone, and the crack was getting low. Casandra got up to go to the bathroom while Dunkin still sat in his chair looking into space high as a kite. As soon as the bathroom door closed Dunkin got up and grabbed her purse, keys, and the rest of the drugs then ran out the door. He got in her car and sped away. Crackhead instincts were beginning to hit Dunkin. He pulled the move he pulled just because he wanted to smoke the rest of the dope by himself.

"What the fuck Dunkin," yelled Casandra as she came out the bathroom and seen that he was gone?

She was used to people running off on her to smoke the rest of the dope when it got low. She wasn't tripping off Dunkin leaving because she had stashed some of her dope on him too. She grabbed her pipe off the table and went in her bedroom to smoke. She noticed her purse and keys were gone but didn't sweat it because she was so high.

After leaving Cassandra's house the only thing on Dunkin's mind was still getting high. He knew he had to be conservative with what he had left because he couldn't go buy it himself and blow his cover. He got on the highway steering the car with his knee while holding the pipe with one hand and the lighter with the other smoking crack while driving. He was listening to John Legend, "all of you" as he drove Cassandra's car dedicating the song to the crack he was smoking. Dunkin now understood why he made so much money selling drugs. He felt better than he ever felt in life so now he felt no one was wrong for smoking dope. In his mind he felt he only had one life to live and he was going to live it to the fullest.

Dunkin was out riding with no destination in mind. He wanted to go spy on a few people, but overall, he just wanted to be alone. All his life he lived to have people around him but at this time he just wanted to have peace. He got off the highway on Emerson Avenue and coasted down the street until he stopped at a McDonald's just to sit in their parking lot and think. Then the thought came to his mind that he needed to get another cellular phone so he could call Abayomi.

Dunkin felt he at least had to call her, but everyone else would just have to wait until he came back around.

Dunkin's family was going crazy trying to figure out where he was at. Of all his years living he had never disappeared on his parents and his sister Tyrea. Since he had never committed an action like this everyone was on edge thinking he was out trying to commit suicide. His children were so worried that they left Aruba and went back home to try to help find their dad. His son Dexter really was feeling some type of way because his dad meant more to him than anyone else on earth. NuNu felt bad for Dunkin, but she was mad as well because it seemed like he loved Milly more than he ever loved her. They all hoped he would surface soon, but just didn't know if he really would.

Dunkin felt he needed to be free for a while before having contact with his family again. The death of Milly was something he wasn't trying to think about. He eventually went back to Cassandra's house after buying a Trac Phone at Family Dollar. Only reason he went back is because he had nowhere else to hide at without somebody noticing him. When he got back Cassandra was so high that she was up wiping the inside of her washer and dryer. She was wiping with a towel and disinfectant spray. For the first time since Milly's death Dunkin could finally laugh. Cassandra looked at him like he was crazy and continued to clean.

While Cassandra was on her knees bent over with her head inside the dryer Dunkin walked up got on his knees, moved her thong to the side and started fucking her from the back. Her moans sounded different because her head was inside the dryer. Dunkin liked the sound because he kept pounding her pussy harder and harder. Cassandra had never had good dick in her whole life, so Dunkin was the best thing that ever happened to her sexually. No matter if they were smoking crack or not, she knew good dick when she felt one.

After he fucked the shit out of her and came so hard in her that she thought the nut was coming up to her throat they went in the bedroom to go to sleep. They were on a crash course from being up for so many days doing drugs. Once they laid down the day was over with for them both. They slept like babies. Cassandra laid her head on his chest and the smell of her hair is really what put Dunkin to sleep. Dunkin knew he had to go face reality one day, but he was going to enjoy his life for the moment.

Meanwhile, Abayomi was in Jamaica on her way to talk to her uncle about Dunkin. She had enough of Dunkin's absence and wanted some answers. She knew in the past he could barely go a day without calling her and now it had been many days, so she was starting to feel worried. Her uncle always had answers, so she was going to holler at him.

"Uncle please help me to find Dunkin. I don't know that he is okay," said Abayomi talking with deep accent as she looked at her uncle.

"That blood clot is the devil my niece. I promised your father that I would never let a man break your heart without me breaking his and that is what I've done to this little boy. You remember when you asked me to keep an eye on him and to scare him away from Indianapolis? I looked into his whereabouts and found that he had a family that didn't consist of you," said her uncle.

"Please tell me that you didn't hurt him. Uncle I love Dunkin and I didn't want you to hurt him. I trust him and I want to spend the rest of my life with him," said Abayomi as she started to cry.

"My dear, you must have forgot that you gave me the order to kill any woman in the middle of you and him, so that he would come back running to you. I didn't want to have his fiancée killed because she was a beautiful woman and I loved watching her naked in the shower. After I had cameras put in their house, I started to watch their actions and that's how I knew he was never going to be with you. He hasn't run back to you yet so he must not really want to be with you," said her uncle.

Her uncle had some of his people that stayed in Indianapolis break into Dunkin and Milly's house and put camera's in every room of their house. Abayomi's father was the leader of a Jamaican gang before his death and left his brother to be the leader when he died. They were based in Jamaica but had the United States on lock too. They had soldiers who were more than willing to die for the gang. He was the one behind the paint ball attack on Dunkin and many other acts of violence on him as well. Dunkin had power, but he wasn't ready for the smoke Abayomi's uncle had for him.

"Well fuck him if he thought he could play me. I want him dead too. Please kill him for me uncle. I've done everything for him I could, and he still played me, I can't live in the same world he lives in anymore, so I want him to go to hell," said Abayomi as she got up and left her uncles voodoo shop in the mall.

"Say no more princess, your wish is my command," said her uncle as he rubbed his hands together with a smile on his face. He loved to kill people. When he would jack off, he would jack off to horror movies because porn didn't get him aroused at all.

Back in Indianapolis Dunkin was waking up from his sleep. Now that he had a few hours of rest he figured he would plot his next move. He concluded that it was time for him to go be back with his family. He looked at Cassandra as she slept and thought about the blessing, she had been for him by letting him stay in her crib like she did. He promised himself again that he would buy her a new house and new car one day soon. He still had money in his pocket from when he went to the bank, so he left it all on her dresser. After that he put on his clothes and left her apartment.

Dunkin left her house with murder on his mind. He didn't know what was going on, but his plan was to get to the bottom of it. Not only had someone killed two of his unborn children with their mothers, but they had attacked him and somehow withdrawn his money from his secret account. He was clueless about everything, but somebody was about to get shook the fuck up.

After walking away from Cassandra's apartment Dunkin pulled out the cellphone he had just bought and called him a ride. He called Terrance to come get him. Terrance told him he was on his way and when Dunkin asked him what had been going on, he just told him he would holler at him in person. He let Dunkin know that the news he was about to hear wasn't good news at all.

Dunkin's son Dexter was out and about with the new love of his life. He had just met her about a month before and had already fallen in love. Dexter was twenty years old with an early college degree and had just lost his virginity to this woman and the pussy had his nose wide opened. He was running and doing whatever she told him to do without a problem. The thing that Dexter didn't know is that she was only with him for one purpose and it wasn't because he came from a wealthy family. She didn't want to meet any of his family. She told him that once they snuck off and got married, she would meet his family then. Dexter was ready for her to be his wife, while she was just postponing time so she could complete some other missions she had in mind.

CHAPTER 13

Terrance hit the corner within minutes to pick up Dunkin. He was driving his old school four door 79' Delta Eighty-Eight, sitting on twenty-eight-inch Rucci rims. From previous experiences with Dunkin he knew Dunkin didn't like riding around in a flashy car. At this time, it was like fuck what Dunkin had to say. Dunkin was lucky Terrance picked up his call anyway. No one else around would have even picked up his call. When he seen Dunkin's facial expression, he knew he wasn't happy with his car of choice for the day. Terrance didn't give a fuck though, Dunkin didn't know, but he didn't have power in the streets like he once had anymore. Terrance was able to stand his ground and keep a section of Nap Town where only he could sell his drugs at. People were standing up for their hoods now and Dunkin wasn't going to be able to go into any hood and lock it down like he did before. Terrance had a twenty-block section on the east side, so he was going to eat regardless. When Dunkin disappeared, he was left to do what he had to do. Dunkin didn't have any power anymore and Terrance had more bad news for him as well. Terrance also thought that Dunkin looked like he had been smoking dope or something then on top of that he had on a Wal Mart outfit and shoes. Dunkin looked like a washed-up crackhead still in denial.

"Damn nigga is this the only car you could have picked out," asked Dunkin as he got in the car with Terrance?

"Shit you called, and I was riding in this. You got other shit to be worried about bro and you're lucky I even came and got you. A lot has changed since you disappeared for your little few days and it look like you been out smoking dope for real nigga," said Terrance as he looked at Dunkin with a serious look on his face. Dunkin was now a marked man in the streets of Indianapolis. The best thing Dunkin could do for himself at this time was get the fuck out of town.

"I guess mathafuckas than grew some balls now in the last few days. You better assume your position nigga; I know that much," said Dunkin as he stared at Terrance.

"Well, the streets are not yours anymore for a start. And for the second somebody has kidnapped your mother and father. Someone has snitched and told a lot of shit, NuNu, Fat Boy, Zynika, and Nicole had a side operation going and got popped off. All of them are locked up with Fed cases. Your kids all disappeared, and your sister disappeared as well. People are claiming their own hood territory now and whoever is the one running things over there decide where they buy their drugs from and they may not choose you," Terrance told him as he avoided telling him that he had his own blocks.

He figured he would keep what he had to himself because he had found a better plug on dope too. He didn't need Dunkin for shit else and only picked him up because he wanted him to know that he still had his back. Terrance planned to help Dunkin with finding his parents no matter what.

"I'm going to attend to all that shit, don't even trip, but you said somebody got my parents. What in the fuck is going on? I can't go with this shit at all. It's not even like I had beef with none of these niggas out here like that. What the fuck going on," asked Dunkin?

"All I can say is that you should have never killed Eric bro, he was the key to finding out everything that is going on. You just got heartless bro and that shit wasn't cool at all. Eric told you that he felt it was a bitch behind this shit and I believe him now more than ever. You have been getting messages saying shit like, Marry Me Or Live In Misery type shit bro and that's some shit a bitch in love will say. The sad part is that I think it may be more than one bitch," said Terrance.

"My nigga I have to get my parents back. Fuck all that other shit," said Dunkin.

"I got you bro and you know that without question. Whoever these weird mathafuckas are that got them seem to FaceTime me every night. They be letting me talk to your moms and pops bro which is some creepy shit to me. At the same time, it makes me feel like it's someone close because it's some emotion behind a person doing some shit like that," said Terrance.

What Dunkin didn't know is that it was NuNu behind his own kids being ambushed in Dexter's house the night they got ruffed up. At first NuNu was going to rob Dunkin by holding her own children for ransom. Then she changed her mind for some reason and decided not to have her people do the ransom job. Instead she had her people go in and tie her children up thinking the situation would make Dunkin spend time with her, but it failed. NuNu knew she would never give up the hope of being with Dunkin, even as she sat in her Federal holding cell. The prosecutors were going to let her go home on house arrest because she didn't have any felony convictions. She was the only one to get a bond from the feds out of all seven of them who were indicted.

"I still have money put up all over the city and left two million in Jamaica with baby, so money isn't the issue. What are they asking for when they call," asked Dunkin?

"That's another funny thing. They don't demand shit at all. They just let me talk to your parents. Your parents will tell me that they are fine and just waiting on you to come back around. Well you can kind of say they're demanding something and that's you. They want you and they don't say what they want you for. I think they think someone is hiding you or something. Then they said you're still posting on Facebook and shit. They said you than put video's up of you fucking bitches and everything," said Terrance.

"I haven't even had my phone to be on Facebook. Somebody than got ahold of my shit and is fucking with me my nigga. I'm a kill whoever behind this shit bro on my momma," said Dunkin.

"Say no more G, as soon as we get the information, we need we will kill them and anyone else we feel like killing. There was a description on the car so we're trying to figure out who was driving the car that day. I told you I'm on it for you bro," said Terrance.

"Appreciate it G. Plenty much," Dunkin said as he reached out to shake up with Terrance.

"And out of all this time I never knew that Zynika and Nicole were both working with NuNu and Fat Boy shooting bricks out of town to like St. Louis or something. They hit though bro, they have them on selling over a hundred bricks in a short period of time. NuNu will be out on house arrest though until the outcome of the case. If I was you, I would stay far away from her when she gets out. I'm hoping none of them will tell on us bro," said Terrance as he put Dunkin up on game.

"I bet they feel real stupid right now. I ain't trippin though I got to get my OG's out of danger," said Dunkin.

"Off top bro and they will be calling here in a while. They usually call around eight every night," said Terrance.

Meanwhile, Tyler which was Lisa's old goon was sitting down at IMPD police headquarters telling everything he knew about Dunkin. Tyler had been trying to catch Dunkin slipping ever since Lisa had died, but he never found him, so he went and told the police on him instead. In Tyler's mind he was feeling like Dunkin should have just married Lisa like she wanted him to. Since he didn't, he was now about to live in misery because Tyler planned to do everything in his power to make Dunkin suffer. Tyler told the detectives and the FBI some key information they needed in order to start investigating Dunkin. They didn't have enough evidence to arrest him or even bring him in for questioning just yet, but they were getting close to putting charges on Dunkin. What they had was enough to get the judge to sign off on wiretaps on Dunkin's and everyone he knew phone lines. What Tyler and law enforcement didn't know is that Dunkin was ready for them because he had no plans of talking on the phone again and was done with the game. Dunkin was going to get his family back to safety and then flee to Jamaica with Abayomi.

Abayomi was still in Jamaica feeling sad. The voodoo spell her uncle put on Dunkin made anyone he loved other than family a possible victim. Then not to mention with the gangsters her uncle had in Indianapolis who did whatever he told them to do. He made Dunkin's life a living hell and though Abayomi was sad she was happy at the same time because

Dunkin thought he was clever enough to play her. Now all she wanted to do was get Dunkin over to Jamaica one more time so she could torture him. When she told her uncle to put some eyes on Dunkin, she never thought her uncle would harm him or his family. She never thought Dunkin was playing her neither so in her eyes they were even.

"Hello," said Abayomi as she prayed, she would hear Dunkin's voice on the other end of the phone.

"Baby, I'm sorry it has been so long. How have you been," asked Dunkin as he felt a sense of relief when he heard Abayomi say hello on the phone?

"Oh my god. Dunkin, I have been so worried about you. I want to say some things to you, but I'm so happy to hear your voice that I can't say anything upsetting to you right now. Please never go that long without calling me again," said Abayomi. All of her harsh feelings went out the window as soon as she heard Dunkin's voice.

"Sweetie, I can't even begin to know where to start with telling you what has been going on, but I am safe now. I have one more big mission to complete and then I'll be over there with you to stay," said Dunkin as he put his forehead into the palm of his hand.

"I will do whatever needs to be done for you to come to me now. Don't waste time, you need to come home with me now," pleaded Abayomi.

She really didn't care nothing about what Dunkin had going on, she just wanted to get him to Jamaica to kill him for trying to make her out of a dummy. Only thing on her mind was making Dunkin suffer. She felt that since he didn't marry her, he would have to live in misery. Her uncle was behind the streets turning against Dunkin. Her uncle had given the word to his people in Indianapolis to sell the streets up by cutting everybody else's prices on all drugs. He knew once people seen that Dunkin wasn't the only one who could have a connect on drugs, they would build themselves up to the point where they would say fuck Dunkin. That's what everyone did too, they said fuck Dunkin. The people who he did wrong were now out to kill him. They wasn't fearing Dunkin at all anymore.

"Don't worry I will tell you everything that has been going on. I won't hold nothing back from you and I have a lot for you to forgive me for, I'm sorry in advance," said Dunkin as he pleaded for forgiveness.

"It is fine my baby; I just want you to be safe. If you want me to come there with you for a while I will. I have my passport." said Abayomi.

For some reason she was ready to forgive Dunkin. She told herself that if he told her the truth about everything, she would have to forgive him. She wasn't the type to hold a grudge after someone came to her with the truth. Abayomi believed in the saying, "the truth will set you free." She knew she would have to go to another country if she forgave Dunkin. That was something she was willing to do because she still loved

Dunkin and wanted to live happily ever after. She knew her uncle would never welcome Dunkin, so she was ready to flee her country before she let her uncle kill him.

"No, just stay where you are at and I will be there in the next few days. Just give me a little time to get things taken care of here," said Dunkin.

Dunkin and Abayomi talked a little more before getting off the phone. They got off the phone with the agreement that Dunkin would be in Jamaica with her within the next four days. Dunkin promised her that he would be there no matter if he finished his business in Indianapolis or not. Dunkin was ready to give up on finding his parents and go away to happiness with the only woman he loved. He felt his parents had lived a very decent life so if they were to die at least they did live a nice and rich life. For once in his life he was putting himself first. Terrance then handed Dunkin the phone to Facetime with his parents,

"Momma are you okay? I promise if anyone touches you, I will find them and kill them."

"I think you should shut the fuck up with the threats before you get your poor little parents here killed," said a person in a KKK gown talking through a voice box to disguise their voice.

"If you want me, I will come with no weapon. Please just let my parents go, they haven't done anything to anyone that's something I promise to you. I'm a man before I'm anything on this earth, I stand on my word and will take responsibility for anything I've done. I just don't want my family in danger," said Dunkin as he looked at the person in the KKK gown on Facetime.

"Well you don't call the shots over here Dunkin. I decide if I want to let your parents go or if I will kill them. How does it feel to not have the power you spoiled ass little punk bitch," asked the person in the gown?

"All I did was ask; I didn't give any demands. I just said what I wanted to happen," replied Dunkin.

"We have to go now," said the person as they hung up the phone before Dunkin could say another word.

When the phone went black Dunkin looked as if he would never see his parents again. At first, he felt he could just skip town and leave without knowing if they were all right or not. After seeing their faces on the phone, he knew he couldn't skip out on his parents. For some reason he just felt there was something familiar about the person on the other side of the phone. He didn't know what it was, but something was making him feel like he knew the person. Though they had on the mask and everything he felt like he knew the person and knew them very well.

Dunkin eventually told Terrance to drop him back off in Castleton Apartments. He figured he would go back over Cassandra's house. Once he told Terrance to drop him off, he immediately thought otherwise. He remembered he had cars parked all over Indianapolis, so he just told him to drop him off to one of his cars. He had him drop him off to one of his most low-key SUV's, it was a 2006 Chevy Tahoe. Dunkin knew he could blend right in with traffic in the Tahoe. Plus, Dunkin remembered he had stashed about forty thousand dollars in the Tahoe as well. He was ready to get the fuck away from Terrance so he could go smoke the pipe.

Once Terrance got Dunkin to his Tahoe, they sat in Terrance's car to talk for a little while. Terrance was surprised with all that Dunkin still had stashed away. Dunkin still had plenty dope, money, properties, and cars. Terrance was beginning to think he made the wrong move by counting Dunkin out. Dunkin then went to look around the inside of his Tahoe just making sure everything he left was still in place. Dunkin had the Tahoe parked on one of his ex-old school chicks' properties. They had never been in a relationship, so she was cool with whatever Dunkin did. Donna was an older woman that didn't look nothing like she was fifty years old. She only hit Dunkin up when she wanted to get dicked down, but other than that Dunkin knew what properties of hers he could go to. Donna had a husband, but she told Dunkin what properties he could use when he needed to. She was cool as hell, but she creeped on her husband because he did his share of creeping as well. No one would have even imagined the things Dunkin had put away and would have got lost trying to find the locations. He was smart when it came to lining things up for his future money wise but was stupid when it came to be making logical decisions.

Before leaving Dunkin told Terrance one more thing and that was to make sure he answered the phone when he called him. He also told him to go check on his house to make sure no one had been in there. Only thing Dunkin wanted to do now was check on

Cassandra and then tend to Milly's family because he knew they were deeply upset about what happened. He knew he couldn't let them know that Milly was dead because of him under no circumstance. Dunkin knew it could possibly start a war if they knew he was the reason she died so he wanted to keep it to himself. He wasn't scared of her family but knew he didn't need any more trouble than what he already had.

Dunkin pulled up to Cassandra's apartment. All her lights were off, but her car was there so he decided to knock on her door anyway. He knocked for about a minute before one of her neighbors came out to talk to him. The neighbor told him that Cassandra had died in her apartment earlier that day and the police believed she died from an overdose. The neighbor told him when Cassandra was found she was naked with a needle still stuck in her arm. Dunkin didn't even know she did heroin.

Dunkin had heard enough. He asked the neighbor if he could tell him of any way to get in touch with her family because he wanted to pay for her funeral. When the guy told him no, Dunkin told him to watch her apartment for whoever would come to get her belongings. Dunkin gave the guy his phone number to give to whoever came. He gave the neighbor that request along with five hundred dollars attempting to let the neighbor know how important his request was. Dunkin then turned Cassandra's doorknob to see if her door was unlocked. It was unlocked so he went in to look around. He seen that Cassandra must have known he left her money because it had been moved. Then he looked around the apartment for crack. He found what looked like two grams of crack and proceeded to smoke it in the apartment in memory of Cassandra.

CHAPTER 14

Dunkin left Cassandra's apartment in the wee hours of the morning and he was high as a kite when he left. Before he left, he was able to get in touch with Cassandra's family and give them more than enough money for Cassandra's funeral. Her family was more than grateful for Dunkin's contribution because they didn't think she had anyone who loved her enough to help. Considering they were only used to her being around broke drug addicts. They promised him they would use the money for the funeral and give the rest to her child. Dunkin told them he would give them money for Cassandra's child every month as well.

Now the only thing on Dunkin's mind was getting in touch with his sister and children. He understood that everyone was spooked when his parents were kidnapped so they disappeared. He still felt they should have left some type of way to be contacted though. Dunkin was thinking selfishly at this time because he forgot he had disappeared too, on top of that he was the first to disappear. He called Terrance and told him to get in touch with his sister and children if there was any way possible.

After a while Dunkin decided he was going to go to his house. He knew it wouldn't be the same without Milly there, but just wanted to go. Nothing about Dunkin was the way it used to be, he had lost weight, his hair was nappy along with his beard, and his mind was all over the place thinking about Milly. Once he got home, he turned off his alarm system and sat down on his couch. He wanted to get his parents back, but at this time it was all about him. Dunkin remembered that he left some cocaine in his room, so he went and got it, then proceeded to the kitchen to cook it into crack. He dry cooked the dope into straight drop. Afterwards he sat back on his plush white leather couch with his feet sank into his four-inch-thick fluffy

Persian rug and smoked his pipe while watching Power on Starz.

Dunkin had some serious thoughts going through his mind at this time. He thought it would be best to kill Terrance. He didn't see why someone would kidnap his parents and let them Facetime with Terrance unless he had something to do with the kidnapping. Then he thought about everyone getting a Fed case except Terrance. Things just weren't adding up in his eyes, so he planned to kill Terrance. The thing Dunkin didn't know is that Terrance was already prepared for him. After Terrance seen Dunkin kill Eric for no reason, he knew to keep his guard up around him.

"Bro, we need to link up as soon as possible. The kidnappers called and said they want to talk to you within an hour and if we are late, they are going to kill your parents," said Terrance as he rushed to talk as soon as Dunkin picked up the phone.

"Come to my house bro," replied Dunkin in an irritated voice.

After hanging up the phone Terrance put his foot on the gas and hurried to get to Dunkin's house. Terrance was just trying to help Dunkin get his parents back. Terrance planned to cut Dunkin all the way off after he helped him bring his parents to safety. At first, Terrance was thinking he would be trading on Dunkin by cutting him off, but then he thought otherwise. Dunkin had turned into another person on Terrance and the man Dunkin turned into was a person Terrance didn't want to be around.

While Terrance was on his way to Dunkin's house, Dunkin was on the phone with Abayomi. They talked about everything going on and Dunkin didn't hold back from telling the truth. She loved the fact that Dunkin was being honest and spilling his heart out to her which she didn't expect. Her father told her when she was young that it wasn't easy for a man to tell the hurtful truth but when he did it meant the love was real. She told Dunkin she didn't want him to come to Jamaica anymore. She told him she instead wanted to meet him in Florida and figure out a destination from there. She made up a story about it being a gang war in Jamaica and said Americans were getting killed rapidly in the war. Abayomi told him not to worry about the two million he had stashed. Since she had business accounts it wasn't hard for her to wash the money through her businesses, plus she already had two million to give him. Dunkin was all with the game plan. Dunkin felt he had three days to get his parents back to safety and on the fourth day he would be with the love of his life. He already imagined sitting on the beach smoking the pipe while watching the waves in the ocean.

Meanwhile, detective Goodfinger was meeting with the FBI getting a plan wrote out so they could get Dunkin off the streets. Their only problem was they had no solid evidence to build a case that would convict Dunkin in court. They knew he sold drugs and knew about multiple murders he committed, but they had no solid proof on anything they knew. Their only way of nailing Dunkin was for them to get NuNu to snitch on him. She was due to be released from Federal holding the next day. They had to give her a reason to snitch on Dunkin. Detective Goodfinger knew getting her to snitch would be hard, but he was still going to try his luck by bringing her in for questioning after her release.

"Look Mr. Goodfinger quit putting this nigger in a category like he is untouchable. We are going to nail this fucking punk," said detective Springwater as she looked at the FBI agents with a look of certainty on her face.

What no one in the room knew was that detective Springwater was another woman in love with Dunkin. She planned to tell him everything going on as soon as she got the chance. If they could persuade

NuNu to snitch on Dunkin, she planned to kill NuNu herself. If you looked at Ms. Springwater, you would have never known she was a detective. She looked good to be in her late forties and her ass stuck out so far that you could use it for a picnic table. Dunkin used to fuck the hell out of her, and the dick made her fall in love. She was a white lady that wouldn't fuck with no man of her race and that made a lot of white men and women hate her, but she didn't give a fuck. She put on a good show for those who didn't know who she really was. She had everyone thinking she was a hardcore detective, but really, she was colder hearted than the criminals she had prosecuted.

Detective Springwater knew about everything going on with Dunkin. She just kept it to herself because she wanted to be the one who helped him find his parents then kill the kidnappers. Tyler was downtown snitching so much that all the officers tried to disappear when they would see him from a distance.

Tyler wanted Dunkin locked up so bad that he couldn't even sleep at night with Dunkin being a free man. Tyler didn't realize the police couldn't go lock Dunkin up just off his word alone. Though they knew his words were true they still had to persuade the Grand Jury. Another thing Tyler didn't know is that detective Springwater was going to kill him before he told anything else.

Dunkin hurried to get his house back proper before Terrance came over. He knew he wouldn't hear the last of it if anyone found out he was smoking crack. What he didn't know is that Terrance already knew deep down in his heart that he had been smoking. Terrance was a hustler and knew a smoker when he seen one. The day Terrance picked up Dunkin he seen Dunkin's fingertips and knew he had been smoking dope. Terrance didn't give a fuck though because he smoked crack himself, though he smoked laced blunts and Dunkin smoked the pipe, it was still crack. Terrance had been smoking on the low for a while and no one ever knew. That's the way he wanted to keep it too.

Dunkin's parents were kidnapped but seemed to not really be in danger. The people who kidnapped them seemed to take care of them for the most part. At times one of them would smack Deacon and call him a stupid cunt but they were cool other than that. His parents were in for the scare of their lives now though. They were tied up in a warehouse that was very big, it looked to be around a million square feet. There was a trash compactor at one of the docks and that's where the kidnappers set up a stand to hold a cellphone. It was about halfway full of trash so it would crush anything between the trash and the mechanical steel plate used to smash the trash together.

"It's time for a field trip," said one kidnapper as he pulled the blind folds off Deacon's and Chelly's eyes.

"What is your problem? What do you want? Just tell us what you want, and we will give it to you so we can go," pleaded Chelly.

"If it was that simple, I would have been an told both of you what was wanted, but it's not that simple. I was paid to do what I'm doing to both of you. The person who paid me seems to not want a ransom or anything like that. What she seems to want is your son Dunkin. She said you two have turned him into a maniac so it will be you two that lure him to her so she can kill him herself," said the kidnapper.

Another kidnapper came from a door about twenty feet away from them with a mask on as well. They untied Deacon and Chelly then put a gun to each of their backs after they told them to stand up slowly. The two were walked to the trash compactor and were told to climb down in it. Deacon and Chelly both hesitated. Then one of the kidnappers grabbed Deacon by the back of the neck and shoved him into the compactor. When Chelly began to cry the other kidnapper grabbed her and told her to do as she was told, promising her if she did, everything would be okay. When she heard that she climbed down in the compactor with her husband. The Love Pink baby blue leggings that outlined the beautiful shape of Chelly sculpted ass was now covered in dirt. They told Chelly and Dunkin to sit in the chairs in front of the trash and to look at the iPhone in front of them.

"Did you obey my command? Is that prick Dunkin around you right now," asked the kidnapper as he looked into the Facetime screen talking to Terrance?

"Yeah, he is right here. Just tell him what the fuck you want," replied Terrance.

"I'm right here and need to know what you want for me to get my parents back," said Dunkin.

"We will drop them off at McDonald's on Emerson by the highway if we can first pick you up at the Burger King on fifty sixth and Emerson," said the kidnapper.

"I'm not putting myself in danger for nobody. My parents have lived their lives and I'm not going to cut my life short because of them," said Dunkin.

"The lady who paid us to do this said you were a piece of shit and I see why she said it. You're a true piece of shit and as soon as I get the chance, I'm going to kill you myself," said the kidnapper as he changed the screen to where Dunkin could now see his parents in the compactor. Three seconds after the kidnapper shifted the camera, he turned the compactor on. Dunkin could then see the steel plate getting closer and closer to smashing his parents.

"Please turn it off. I will come there to meet you," pleaded Dunkin as he put his pride to the side.

"Be there in forty-five minutes no later than that," demanded the kidnapper.

Dunkin had Terrance drop him off at the Burger King where the kidnappers demanded him to go. The kidnappers made a deal that as soon as Dunkin got inside the back of their van, they would drop his parents off to the McDonald's and the kidnappers kept their word. Dunkin's parents were now worried about him. They heard when Dunkin tried to shrug off the kidnappers' request at first but seen how he changed his mind when he seen the compactor. They knew Dunkin would never leave them in danger. In their hearts they knew Dunkin would talk shit to anybody before giving up.

The kidnappers took Dunkin to the same warehouse his parents had just left. Instead of sitting him by the docks like they did his parents they took Dunkin to an expensively decorated bedroom. They gave him towels then told him body wash and everything else he needed was in the bathroom already. They told him he had a half an hour to shower and shave or they were told to shoot him in his head no question. Dunkin didn't waste any time before he took the towels and went into the bathroom. Dunkin was surprised at the way the bathroom looked. Someone had really taken their time out to perfect the all burgundy, green, and gold decorations in the bathroom. It had a jacuzzi tub big enough to fit at least fifteen people inside. Dunkin thought it was something like his, but it was even better. Dunkin just found it weird that all his favorite hygiene items were already in the bathroom. He wondered how whoever it was knew what he liked when it came to hygiene.

As soon as thirty minutes were up a voice through an intercom speaker told Dunkin to dry off and go lay in the bed naked. Dunkin followed the order and went to lay down. The room was very dark, the only light that came in the room was from the sky light in the ceiling. He laid back and wondered what the fuck was going on and why the fuck they wanted him to lay down. Then the men came back in the room and tied his arms to the upper bed posts and his legs to the lower bed posts. The posts stood about five feet high off the ground. The mattress was about fourteen inches thick and the room was so comfortable that Dunkin was ready to fall asleep. After laying in the bed about five minutes Dunkin did fall asleep.

Dunkin woke up to his dick being sucked by a masked woman. She had turned on the lights in the room, but it was still so dim that he couldn't tell the identity of the woman. He could see that she was masked up with only her mouth exposed. Everything else on her body was butt naked. He felt she was sucking his dick good but really didn't know what she was doing. In a way he didn't mind getting kidnapped to get raped by a thick ass woman. After she gave him head for a few minutes she turned around and planted her body on him in the sixty-nine position. Dunkin went to work immediately going from eating her pussy to eating her ass. He could see the view of her ass in his face and it made his dick hard just by looking at it. He had never seen such a pretty firm ass in his life. He ate her pussy and ass so good that she couldn't even suck his dick as he ate away at both holes. She just laid her head on his dick and moaned. Dunkin was enjoying eating her out because her ass was so perfect, and she smelled so fresh.

After he got done eating her out, she climbed on top of him and put the head of his dick in her pussy. Her pussy was so tight that he didn't think his dick would fit in, but then her pussy started to drip, and his dick started to enter her little by little. After it got so far in, he came to a barrier and that let him know he was having sex with a virgin. Then all types of thoughts started to go through his mind. His mind was all over the place as the woman now started to bleed and ride his dick even harder. She rode his dick until he emptied all the sperm in his nut sack in her and he felt good as he released. After that the woman laid next to him and started to kiss him.

"You have to be kidding me. Get the fuck off me you're a crazy bitch," said Dunkin as he tried with every muscle in his body to take the restraints off him.

"What you always acted like this is what you wanted ever since I was a kid. Now you got it and you act like this. You have run off every man who has ever tried to get close to me and I felt it was because you wanted me yourself. Was it good to you daddy," asked his sister Tyrea as she grabbed his dick and started to giggle?

"You are one sick bitch and you better let me out of here now," said Dunkin.

"No, you shut the fuck up right now Dunkin before I kill you," said Tyrea as she elbowed Dunkin in the face.

"I don't care you will just have to kill me. I should have known something wasn't right when I saw the so-called kidnappers Facetime Terrance and not give a request for money. Bitch you got off on this one, but I promise I will kill you. You are my fucking sister and you just fucked me acting like you really liked it. You're a sick bitch I can't believe you," said Dunkin.

"I always thought you wanted me Dunkin. I thought this is what you wanted," cried Tyrea.

"Look how dumb you sound. Why in the fuck would I want to fuck my own sister? I am so disgusted with myself that I want to just kill myself," said Dunkin.

"I thought you knew this whole time that we are not real sister and brother. You were adopted and that's why mom and dad always understand you and protect you even when you're wrong. Moms sister left you out in the trash after giving birth to you then mom got you and never let you go. You are not really my brother, you're my cousin," said Tyrea as she tried to lie to Dunkin.

"Bitch you're fucking lying. Untie me right now. I know who the fuck my parents are, you can't try to run that shit on me. You're just a sick bitch, if I was your cousin, you're still wrong," said Dunkin.

"I'll untie you and let you leave if you want, but I'm telling you now that if you don't leave with me and get married, you'll live in misery the rest of your life. I have loved you ever since we were kids. You always protected me and told me how beautiful I was. I can't believe you're acting like you don't want me. I have saved myself for you all my life. Yes, I lied we are brother and sister, but we can just leave everything and everyone else behind, get married, and live in another country. We have all the money we need we won't want for nothing. I bought this warehouse we are in and have a few more. I've been buying and selling them for years now and none of you even knew about it. I did it to save money because I knew one day we would fall in love and run away forever," said Tyrea as she went ahead and untied Dunkin.

"I than already fucked so I may as well fuck you again the right way," said Dunkin as he was untied.

As soon as he was untied, he started to tongue kiss Tyrea and then kissed her all over her body. Then he got on top of her and fucked her nice and slow. He told her that her virginity should have never been taken with her riding a dick. He told her the way he was now fucking her was the way her virginity should have been taken. He made love to her for every bit of thirty minutes before busting a nut inside her again.

After they had sex again Dunkin got up to leave. Tyrea begged him for a relationship, but Dunkin told her he couldn't live with himself after having sex with his sister. He told her he was leaving Indianapolis for good in an hours' time and would never look back. Dunkin told Tyrea that he would be leaving the country with Abayomi after he met up with her in Florida.

"I will see you again my love, I don't want no other man, but you," said Tyrea as she started to cry like a baby.

Dunkin walked away from the warehouse in disgust. He couldn't believe he had just had sex with his own sister. Then he thought about the fact that she practically told him to marry her or live in misery. Dunkin then knew that Tyrea had been weird all the years of her life because she was crazy as fuck. He was mad at himself for having sex with her again after he was forced to the first time. Then he thought about the fact that he would have to have her killed if she came up pregnant.

Tyrea's warehouse was in Plainfield, Indiana and Dunkin was lucky it was by a bus terminal connector so he could catch the city bus to Indianapolis. His mind was all over the place and he just wanted to get away from everyone and be at peace. While on his bus ride Terrance called him and told him that NuNu had gotten out of jail. He wondered why Terrance would have called him and he knew he was supposed to be kidnapped. That's when Dunkin came up with the idea to sneak up on Terrance and kill him. He just knew something was fishy about Terrance though he didn't know exactly what it was.

While Dunkin was on the Indygo bus Tyrea was back at the warehouse crying and cuddled in the bed smelling the part of the bed Dunkin had just got up from. She turned on her TV that Dunkin didn't even know was there. She had put surveillance in Dunkin's and Milly house a long time ago and was watching Dunkin take showers and have sex with Milly for months and months. She had everything recorded just like Abayomi's uncle did. Her plan was to watch them with Dunkin and tell him about the first time when she knew she was in love with him, but he left her mad and heartbroken.

While Abayomi thought she was the cause of Milly's death. She really wasn't at all. When her uncle put the hit out on Milly in the hospital his soldiers never got a chance to carry out the hit. It was Tyrea who had scrubs and knew all about the hospital and medicines. When Milly saw her come in her hospital room, she was happy to see her stepsister. Tyrea greeted her and told her she was told to come replace her IV with more medicine, but really put a fatal concoction in her IV bag to kill her. Abayomi's uncles' soldiers didn't tell him that Milly was dead when they got there, so they could still collect the payment for the hit. Tyrea was also the one with the KKK gown on who changed Dunkin's music while he was showering. She was waiting for him to come home on the couch naked, but then got scared and didn't get out in time before he got home. That's when she decided to watch him take a shower and fuck with him. She wore the KKK gown because she knew about people wearing them and fucking with

Dunkin. Tyrea knew way more about what was going on than anyone else. The night she killed Lisa she did it because she didn't want Dunkin having no more babies by anyone except her. The innocent Tyrea was behind both of Dunkin's baby mama's being killed and carried the murders out on her own.

CHAPTER 15

When Dunkin got off the bus in downtown Indianapolis, he decided to go to Circle Centre mall to look at some clothes and grab some food. He stayed there for about an hour before Terrance picked him up. Dunkin never told him what happened. Whenever Terrance asked him about the situation, he just told him that everything was fine. Terrance found that odd but didn't really give a fuck because Dunkin was okay. Terrance told Dunkin that NuNu had been released from federal custody until trial or a plea bargain was signed. Terrance told him that he should stay away from her because he knew the police was watching her very closely.

Dunkin informed Terrance that he wanted to get dropped off at home so he could pack and head to Florida. Terrance didn't argue with him he told Dunkin he was doing the best thing for his life by getting away from Indianapolis. Dunkin told him that he wasn't scared of nothing or no one, but he just needed time to get away and think. He didn't even want to go see his parents before leaving and had no intentions of ever seeing them again in life. After having sex with his own sister, he just wanted to go and never come back.

Once Dunkin got home, he sat back on his couch for a few minutes thinking about how quick he had to get out of the house because it felt empty without Milly being there with him. He knew he didn't go to her funeral neither so that made him feel bad as well. Terrance was the only one other than his sister who knew he was going to Florida, but neither of them knew where he would be going after that. Dunkin himself didn't even know where he was going to go. He just knew he wanted to talk to his children and then leave Indianapolis for good. Dunkin planned on leaving all his properties and businesses to his children, but he had something very special for his youngest boy Dexter. Of all his children Dexter was his favorite and his other children knew that. Dexter was his favorite because he always had money on his mind and had so much pride that he didn't ask nobody for nothing. Dunkin was going to give Dexter his house to do whatever he wanted to do with it.

Dunkin got a little hungry and decided to make him a toasted peanut butter and jelly sandwich. Once he was done eating, he was still hungry so he figured he would go to Wendy's to get him something to eat. He walked out to his six-car garage and decided to drive Milly's Bentley coupe. He then asked himself what he would do with all their cars and everything else they had in the house. That's when he said to himself, he would just keep the house and not give it to Dexter. He knew he would never be able to figure out who to give things to, so he just wanted to leave everything where it was at.

"Yeah, let me get that four-dollar meal with spicy nuggets, ranch, and a fruit punch to drink no ice.

Shit let me get a small chili too with cheese and sour cream," said Dunkin as he talked into the microphone in the Wendy's drive thru.

"Okay, will that be all for you sir," asked the clerk?

"Yeah that's it," replied Dunkin.

"Pull around for your total, sir," said the clerk.

After Dunkin got his food, he parked in the parking lot to eat. He finished his food quick and just sat there to think for a while. He heard what sounded like a cellular phone notification coming from Milly's glove box and opened it to find an iPhone he never knew Milly had. After touching the home button, he seen that the phone had no screen lock on it, so he started to look through the phone. He seen correspondence between Milly and a person he didn't know. Dunkin was shocked at what he seen. He seen that Milly was behind the attack on his stash house, but she never intended for anyone to get killed. He seen that Milly was behind the purchases made from his bank account as well. He just didn't understand how someone as innocent as Milly could plot some shit like that. He then seen another conversation between her and the same person. This time Milly was telling the person that she just wanted Dunkin to love her like she loved him. She told the person that she wanted him to hurt and she be the only one there with him to heal him so that he would know she always had his back.

After seeing the messages Dunkin got mad all over again. He couldn't believe that Milly was the reason Draco was dead. Dunkin just didn't understand why everyone had worn KKK gowns while doing attacks on him if none of them knew what each other was doing. He was lost for words and now all he wanted to do was go home and smoke the rest of the little crack he had left. His plan was to go to the airport after that. Dunkin knew his life would never be normal in Indianapolis, so he just wanted to leave.

As soon as Dunkin got home, he fired up his pipe and decided to take a shower. He got in the shower and turned on his shower TV to a porn video. He stood in the shower jacking off and once he was finished, he took his shower. He stayed in the shower for about an hour enjoying the hot water and the steam that came off the water. Dunkin knew the shower he was taking would be the last shower he took at his house for a very long time. He knew Abayomi wouldn't have minded moving to Indianapolis, but he didn't want to put her in a bad situation. After seeing that Milly was on some bullshit Dunkin no longer had the love for her that he once did. If all the beef wasn't going on with him in Indianapolis, he would have moved Abayomi right into his house and said fuck Milly's memories.

"What do you want," asked Dunkin as he answered his Facetime call from his sister Tyrea?

"Just like I had you kidnapped that time I can do it again so watch how you talk to me," answered Tyrea.

"Can you just please tell me what you want," asked Dunkin?

"I want you Dunkin. Don't act like that with me. I'm trying my best to show you that I love you and will do anything for you. I'm the one who took Lisa and Milly out of your life and I did it because I knew they didn't deserve you. This is the fucking thanks I get after trying to make your life safe," said Tyrea.

"You are one crazy bitch and I need you to leave me the fuck alone. I will come and kill you right now. You're not my sister anymore and never call this phone again," said Dunkin as he looked in his sister eyes through the phone screen. That's when he seen his sister cry and all he could think to himself was that she was a crazy ass bitch.

"You punk ass bitch I will see you soon and I promise I will kill you this time I tried to give you a chance to do the right thing. The cops are already looking for you anyway. You should have never raped me, I'm your sister Dunkin. You raped me and you will go to prison for it," said Tyrea.

Dunkin got off the phone with his sister in disbelief. The only thing on his mind now was getting the fuck away. He had money put away all around his house, so he grabbed a duffel bag and walked around the house filling it up with money from his secret stashes. After filling his bag up with money, he made him a glass of tea and decided to sit down on the couch to calm his thoughts. He got a call from his parents and they told him the police had come to their house looking for him. They told him they never wanted to talk to him again because he raped Tyrea. While they were saying that he was already grabbing the keys to his Range Rover and heading to his garage with his luggage in hand. He was stopped short when he recognized a note with his name on it. It was a note that Milly must have wrote right before she was attacked in their home. She told him in the note that sometimes you could find love in the oddest places and she just wanted to share her love with him.

Tears started to come from his eyes as he walked back in the house to sit on his couch. As tears rolled down his face, he pulled out his cellular phone and started to play Spades Plus. He had to do something to get his mind off Milly. His life had turned into a true problem over the last few weeks and he didn't know what to think. He started to think that maybe he shouldn't have killed Eric because he always had a way of putting things in a better way for him to understand. His thoughts were knocked short when he was hit in the head with a vase. It was a hollow vase so there was no blood, but he was knocked out for sure.

Tyrea was now in the hospital talking to detectives about being raped by Dunkin. They pulled his semen from her vaginal area, plus she had cut her face and blacked her own eye. Her parents were there with her, but they both thought something was funny about the whole situation. It didn't matter what her parents thought though because the police were all for her story. It was victim impact people there to support her and everything. News stations came out to interview her and Dr. Lawson had just received an email about her situation. Tyrea being raped by her own brother was a very big deal to people, especially being that he had taken her virginity as well. Tyrea even went into detail about Dunkin killing his best friend Dizzy. Now the detectives were looking for him for rape and murder.

Nunu was now out of jail and looking for Dunkin. The only thing on her mind was staying free. She wanted to meet with Dunkin to tell him the feds were all over him and that he needed to stay away from everyone. The feds had already offered her a deal if she was to tell on Dunkin. Nunu didn't want to tell on him, but if he didn't want to marry her then she was going to tell. Her thoughts were that he was going to marry her or live in misery because she knew Dunkin couldn't handle prison. If he did marry her though she was going to take her charge and do her little couple years in prison. All she wanted was Dunkin and that was it.

Dunkin woke up in an unfamiliar basement with no one around him. He was strapped down to a chair. All he could do was think. There was no sound at all where he was at and no light shined upon him. He thought it was odd that there were no windows, but his mind was really on who the fuck had him where he was at. He was starting to get hungry so he was hoping that whoever it was would give him something to eat before killing him or whatever they were going to do.

Nunu was meeting up with Terrance to talk to him about what was going on with the case. Terrance was looking for Dunkin to go with him, but there was no answer, so he went by himself. They met up at Starbucks because that's where Nunu wanted to meet up at. Nunu was still down for the hustle. She knew where all Fat Boy's money was at plus all his drugs and she planned to take it all. After Nunu and Terrance had a talk they left each other with the agreement that they would be partners no matter if Dunkin was involved or not.

After leaving from meeting up with NuNu Terrance went to grab him a Gyro from Jordan's Fish and Chicken. He sat in the parking lot eating his food while listening to music. He was so into eating his food that he didn't see the black Monte Carlo pull to the side of him with an AK 47 hanging out the window. They shot Terrance over forty times with the high-powered assault rifle. They left him there dead with a piece of his Gyro hanging out his mouth and some fries with ketchup on them in his hand.

Nunu had lured Terrance to the Starbucks only to have him killed. When he left the Starbucks, he was followed all the way to Jordan's Fish and Chicken. Nunu had her cousins from Chicago come to

Indianapolis to do the hit. She needed Terrance out the way because she didn't want Dunkin to have anyone around him who would make him feel comfortable. She wanted to be the only one who Dunkin felt like he had other than his children. If Dunkin still didn't want to be with her after that she was going to send him to prison or the grave. Nunu was on some shit and she wasn't taking no for an answer from nobody.

Dunkin was awakened by the smell of bleach. After being locked down in the basement for what seemed like an eternity someone was finally down there. He was surprised by who he was looking at, but just didn't know he was in for an even bigger surprise. Dunkin knew he was in for some bullshit as soon as he seen her face. He didn't give a fuck though he felt everything that could go bad had already went bad so nothing else was a surprise to him.

"Wake up pretty boy Floyd," said the woman as she stood there looking sexy as hell naked in front of

Dunkin. All she had on was red high heels and red lipstick.

"Bitch fuck you. I should have known it was something with you bitch," said Dunkin as he talked to the woman, he met the night he bought his whole crew Corvette's at the Roof Top bar downtown Indianapolis.

"How rude are you, wow," asked Alexis as she laughed at Dunkin and smeared her ass into his face? Her butt cheeks separated as she rubbed her asshole up and down his nose and giggled.

After that Alexis went to the corner of the basement and grabbed a stun gun. She walked up to Dunkin and stunned him on the nose. Dunkin felt the pain, but he didn't cry or let her know that it bothered him. He sat there like a soldier who wasn't going to fold. She just stared at him like he was crazy as she thought of a way, she could make him cry. For some reason Dunkin still turned her on, but he was so strong to her that she wanted to see him weak.

"I know you're wondering why you're here. The thing is that you played the wrong woman. You're a fucking dog and I was paid to get you in this basement you're in now. The sex was great, but I only fucked you because I was drunk," said Alexis.

"Fuck you bitch," said Dunkin as he tried to spit on her before she smacked the shit out of him.

"Well since you want to be a smart ass, I won't say her name I'm just going to tell her to come down here and when she does if you do anything to disrespect her I promise I'll burn you alive. You have put her through enough and she happens to be my cousin," said Alexis.

After she said that the basement door opened, and India came walking down the stairs. When Dunkin seen her his eyes got big and he couldn't say a word. India looked at him and smiled, but she almost untied him and let him go. When she laid eyes on Dunkin the love, she once had for him came back all at once. She was too deep in love with her new man to go there with Dunkin though. She knew when Dunkin seen her new man, he would try to break his restraints and kill her, but she didn't care. She had just recently fell in love with her new man and he was the first man she loved other than Dunkin. She never thought that could happen, but it did.

"I bet you're surprised to see me huh, it has been a long time," said India. Dunkin just looked down in embarrassment because he knew he was wrong for messing around with Lisa after India disappeared.

"Nigga you heard what the fuck she just said didn't you," asked Alexis as she smacked Dunkin and grabbed his chin to make him look up at India?

"Bitch why don't you just shut the fuck up sometimes," answered Dunkin.

"I wish I could, but I want you to respect her and know that what you did to her was wrong," said Alexis.

“Yeah it’s a surprise. I thought you were dead all this time,” said Dunkin as he looked at India.

“Thought I was dead then go and fuck my best friend. I’m glad somebody killed that bitch before I could get ahold of her,” said India. Her language surprised Dunkin because she didn’t even cuss the last time, he seen her.

CHAPTER 16

India stood there as her, and Dunkin looked each other in the eye. Alexis had already left, but she gave Dunkin some head before she left. She promised him it would be the last time his dick would ever be sucked by anyone. Dunkin's dick couldn't even get hard because of the situation, but that didn't stop Alexis from going in on him anyway. India stared Dunkin in his eyes while Alexis was giving him head and all Dunkin could do was think about how bad he had fucked up. India had outsmarted Dunkin in every angle of the game, and no one was ever able to do Dunkin like that. He figured she must have been mapping some shit out for the years she was gone.

"So, you raped your own sister? And you're the one who killed Dizzy," asked India as she looked at her phone in disbelief?

"I didn't do none of that shit. And fuck you if you want to believe that shit. Who the fucked told you that," asked Dunkin as he tried to break loose from his restraints?

"Well it's all over the news. It's about to come on in a minute and I'll let you see it for yourself," said India as she shifted her phone to a wider view and put it in front of Dunkin.

When the news came back on Dunkin knew if he made it out of the basement, he would still be going to prison for the rest of his life. He couldn't believe it was his own sister setting him up that way. When she told him he better marry her, or he was going to be living in misery she was right.

"This is Eric Snipwalker with Fox 59 news. There is a warrant out for a man by the name of Dunkin Houston for rape and murder. He is also the prime suspect in the disappearance of a lady by the name of India Reeves a few years back. Mr. Houston is said to be armed and extremely dangerous. He is a king pin drug dealer with a lot of money and has close ties to other countries. If you see him, please don't approach him as he is armed and dangerous. The DEA, FBI, IMPD, and ATF offices have been investigating him for some time now but were never able to get any rock-solid proof on him. They now have proof and just need his body so they can make an arrest. He is known to be a charmer to women, so lady's please think with your mind instead of your pussy if he approaches you. Looks can be deceiving and he sure is, so please watch yourselves. He is also the suspect in many other murders across Indianapolis and surrounding areas," said the newscaster as Dunkin looked at India's phone.

Dunkin now knew he was in for some serious shit. He really wasn't tripping though because he had enough money in cash to last him a lifetime if he were to move to Africa. He knew he would have a problem getting to his safe deposit box to get deeds and titles to his houses and cars, but it wasn't nothing he couldn't manage. His main priority was now getting the hell out of the basement he was confined to. His thoughts were about his children and the fact that he knew he would never be able to talk to them again. He was also upset because he wouldn't be able to give them the gifts, he had for them and see the smiles on their faces once he gave them their gifts. He was imagining the smile that would have been on his favorite child's face Dexter when he was to tell him he was going to give him his house after he had his things moved from it.

"It looks like you're in some deep shit here sir and you deserve it. You played me like a fool for too long and that's why I disappeared on you. I really could have killed you a long time ago, but I waited until the right time. You are a fucking loser and you are about to suffer for not marrying me even after you told me you would on many occasions. My children haven't seen me nor have my family seen me because of you. I left because of you Dunkin and I was repaid by you fucking my slut ass best friend and getting her pregnant. There is nothing you could ever say to me again in life. And to think I was ready to forgive you when I first came in this basement and laid eyes on you. I guess that's just silly me you are a fucking fool," said India.

Alexis came back in the basement still butt naked. She pulled out a razor and cut every piece of clothing Dunkin had on him off. Then she turned on Megan Thee Stallion's song "Hot girl summer" and started to twerk. Dunkin looked and wished he was in a different situation with Alexis because her ass just jiggled and jiggled, and she was sexy as fuck to him. He knew Alexis really liked him because she gave him head even while he was in restraints. After the song went off Alexis went into combat mode and started to beat the shit out of Dunkin. The only thing he enjoyed about the beating is when she put her pretty toes in his mouth but got mad when she told him she dipped them in a toilet full of piss before coming back to the basement.

"Please stop beating him. That's enough," said India as she stopped Alexis from beating Dunkin.

"So, you are showing mercy for this nigga after everything his bitch ass did to you? This punk ass nigga should be suffering right now. If you don't want him to suffer then just pay me my fucking money and I will leave this fucking house right now," said Alexis as she screamed at India.

"Your money is in the cabinet upstairs just get it and leave Alexis," said India as she looked at Dunkin while starting to cry. Dunkin looked at her feeling like he might have a chance to persuade her to let him go, but what he didn't know is that everything her and Alexis was doing was already planned out.

"Please let me go India. I promise to disappear and never come back. You know I loved you for all the years we were together. I was just thinking with my dick instead of my true feelings. I know you still love me and that's why you stopped her from beating me.

Please let me go," said Dunkin as he pleaded for India to let him go.

"You know a long time ago I would have fell for that, but the new woman I am now won't let me fall for your bullshit," said India as she jumped not expecting Alexis to throw a basketball at Dunkin's head.

"And you still want to try to run game on my cousin. You don't love her and never did. That's why it was so easy for you to start fucking her best friend. I wish I could have killed that bitch my damn self," said Alexis.

"Bitch you stay out of this; I know my baby still loves me. You don't know our history," said Dunkin as he tried to sound persuasive to India.

"Well sure, but I don't think her new man will appreciate you trying to make his woman out of a fool again," said Alexis.

"Fuck her new man he's not half the man I am. I bought India everything she could have possibly wanted when we were together. The only problem I had was cheating. I never laid a hand on her or nothing. So, fuck you Alexis and fuck whoever the nigga is too," said Dunkin.

"No nigga it's fuck you. You're not half the man I am or half the man I'm still going to become. You have to pay for breaking my woman's heart," said the man as he stormed down the basement stairs and hit Dunkin in his mouth.

"You got to be kidding me. Not my own son. Not my Dexter," said Dunkin as he looked his son in his eyes. He couldn't believe his own son had just went against him for some pussy.

"Yeah it's me nigga," said Dexter. Dunkin had never heard Dexter talk like he was talking.

"Dexter you better untie me right now. Your mother would kill you if she knew you had me down here like this," said Dunkin.

"This is my woman and I go with whatever she says. In the bible it says that a man who finds a wife finds a good thing and is favored by the Lord. I must put my woman before you and my mother. Shit look at all the bitches you put before your own kids. I remember you not showing up to parent teacher conferences and all that shit because you would be laid up with a bitch and shit. You giving us money didn't replace the time you never spent with us. You are a worthless piece of shit and you're just mad because I know how to appreciate my woman and you didn't when you had her. I put all this shit together to get your punk ass down here and I'm about to make you suffer for breaking my woman's heart," said Dexter.

"If I get loose, I promise I'm going to kill all you bitches, especially you Dexter. I knew your ass was soft you punk ass little boy. I thought you would grow up and be gay you fag ass nigga. Do you fuck her, or do she fuck you, you bitch ass boy," asked Dunkin as he tried to spit on all three of them? When he did that Alexis stunned him in the mouth with the stun gun.

"You going to learn to keep your spit to yourself," said Alexis while she was shocking him with her stun gun.

"So, I'm a fag huh," asked Dexter as he started to unbutton his pants?

After Dexter unbuttoned his pants, he pulled India closer to him and they started to kiss. There was already an air up mattress in the basement, so they laid down on it. Dexter and India both got naked in front of Dunkin and made love to each other. India sucked Dexter's dick and he ate her pussy and sucked her toes. India was the one who showed Dexter how to make love. Dunkin just watched wishing he could get loose and kill them. While they were making love, Alexis was watching them and playing with her pussy. Next thing you knew Alexis was squirting all over the place and made sure she squirted some right in Dunkin's face.

"I laid that dick on her to be a fag huh. I'm tired of seeing your face it's time to have a little fun with you. You always wanted to be the boss of everyone, now you're sitting there looking like a bitch," said Dexter as he went back up the stairs.

When Dexter came back down the stairs, he had two five-gallon buckets with him. They were both filled with super glue. He told Alexis and India to go back upstairs and get the box he had sitting at the top of the stairs. Dexter had put his clothes back on, but India and Alexis were still walking around naked. Dunkin just didn't know what was about to happen to him.

"Do what you have to do fag boy I've never been a bitch and never will be," said Dunkin.

"Oh, I bet you're going to scream after this, and we will see who the fag is then. You oh fake ass Prince looking chump," said Dexter as he began to laugh.

When the ladies came back down the stairs, they came with a box full of rats. There was at least thirty rats in the box. You could hear them trying to scratch their way out of the box. Dunkin didn't know what he was in for, but it didn't look good for him. Dexter poured the superglue on Dunkin's head and let it drip down as he grabbed the rats one by one and began to glue them to Dunkin's head as he laughed. The ladies didn't know what Dexter had up his sleeve but they liked what they were seeing as they seen the fear in Dunkin's eyes and almost heard him say "please stop" before Dexter put the back half of a rat in Dunkin's mouth before gluing his mouth shut. Dunkin now had the ass of a rat in his mouth.

After that Dexter poured the rest of the glue on Dunkin's body as he was still strapped to the chair and threw rats at his body as they stuck to him like he was a baseball player catching baseballs.

"I know I can make you scream but I'd rather you eat a rat's ass and suffer," said Dexter. The rats on Dunkin were trying to get loose but they were stuck.

After Dexter said that he smacked India and Alexis on their asses and told them to go upstairs. When he smacked them on their asses both of their asses jiggled, and they started to twerk. Dexter followed them up the stairs. Once Dexter was at the top of the stairs, he grabbed another box. It was five Python snakes in the box. He held the box and quickly flung the snakes out the box and into the basement before turning out the basement light and dead bolting the door shut.

"Baby, I told you I would make him suffer. You are my queen and I will put no one above you. Let's see if his punk ass makes it out of this situation. Those snakes bite humans too, but really going to tear his ass up with all those live rats glued to him," said Dexter as he started to laugh.

"He could have never been the man you are. Now bring your ass in here and fuck both of us," said India as her and Alexis both started trying to rip Dexter's clothes off him.

THE END

Contact me for book signings, speaking engagements, or just some uplifting words at:

ericw8403@gmail.com

Made in the USA
Middletown, DE
29 December 2021

57212675R00184